To Nicole
love Eleanor

About the Author

Eleanor Agnes Berry is the author of 20 published books and says her first brush with literature was when she broke windows in Ian Fleming's house at the age of eight. 'He struck me as being a singularly disagreeable man, with no understanding of children,' she recalls. Of Welsh ancestry, she was born and bred in London. She holds a BA Hons degree (a 2:2) in English.

Eleanor specialises in black humour. The works of Gorki, Dostoevsky, Gogol, Edgar Allan Poe and James Hadley Chase have strongly influenced her writings. While at university she completed an unpublished contextual thesis on the Marquis de Sade (whom she refers to as 'de Soggins'). In her spare time she wrote a grossly indecent book, entitled *The Story of Paddy,* which she had the good sense to burn, and inadvertently set a garage on fire.

After leaving university she worked as a commercial translator, using French and Russian. She then worked as a research assistant to a Harley Street specialist and has since worked intermittently as a medical secretary. She was unfairly sacked from St Bartholomew's Hospital in London because she had been a close friend of the late Robert Maxwell's. (She had worked there for five years!)

Two of her novels are available in Russian and a third, which she refrains from naming, is currently being made into a film. This is her tenth book to be published by Book Guild Publishing.

Eleanor is the author of numerous articles in *The Oldie* magazine and has appeared on television and on radio several times, inlcuding Radio California. Her interests include Russian literature, Russian folk songs, Irish rebel songs, the cinema, amateur piano playing, sensational court cases, the medical profession, entertaining her nephews, and swimming across Marseille harbour for kicks. When she dies, she will have her ashes scattered over Marseille harbour, her favourite place.

Eleanor is the maternal niece of the late, famous, self-confessed gypsy author, Eleanor Smith, after whom she was named. Sadly, Eleanor Smith died before Eleanor was born.

D1489857

Books by Eleanor Berry

Tell Us a Sick One Jakey (A black comedy about a mortuary
    attendant who dies of a brain tumour. Out of print.)
Never Alone with Rex Malone
The Ruin of Jessie Cavendish (available in Russian)
Your Father Died on the Gallows (two editions) (available in
    Russian)
Someone's Been Done Up Harley
O, Hitman, My Hitman!
The Revenge of Miss Rhoda Buckleshott
The Most Singular Adventures of Eddy Vernon
Take It Away, It's Red!
Stop the Car, Mr Becket! (formerly *The Rendon Boy to the Grave
    Is Gone*)
Robert Maxwell as I Knew Him
Cap'n Bob and Me
McArandy was Hanged on the Gibbet High
The House of the Weird Doctors
Sixty Funny Stories
The Most Singular Adventures of Sarah Lloyd
Alandra Varinia – Sarah's Daughter
The Rise and Fall of Mad Silver Jaxton
By the Fat of Unborn Leopards
The Killing of Lucinda Maloney

Reviews

Tell Us a Sick One Jakey
'This book is quite repulsive!' Sir Michael Havers, Attorney General

Never Alone with Rex Malone
'A ribald, ambitious black comedy, a story powerfully told.' Stewart Steven, *The Daily Mail*

'I was absolutely flabbergasted when I read it!' Robert Maxwell

The Ruin of Jessie Cavendish
'Eleanor Berry is to Literature what Hieronymus Bosch is to Art. As with all Miss Berry's books, the reader has a burning urge to turn the page.' Sonia Drew, *The International Continental Review*

Your Father Died on the Gallows
'A unique display of black humour which somehow fails to depress the reader.' Craig McLittle, *The Rugby Gazette*

'This book is an unheard of example of English black humour. Eleanor Berry is almost a reincarnation of our own beloved Dostoevsky.' Sergei Robkov, Russian magazine, *Minuta*

Robert Maxwell as I Knew Him
'One of the most amusing books I have read for a long time. Eleanor Berry is an original.' Elisa Segrave, *The Literary Review*

'Undoubtedly the most amusing book I have read all year.' Julia Llewellyn-Smith, *The Times*

'With respect and I repeat, with very great respect, because I know you're a lady, but all you ever do is just go on and on and on and on about this bleeding bloke,' Reginald Kray.

Cap'n Bob and Me
'A comic masterpiece.' *The Times*

'As befits the maternal granddaughter of F.E. Smith (famous barrister who never lost a case) Eleanor Berry has a sharp tone of phrase and a latent desire for upsetting people. Campaigning for her hero, Robert Maxwell, in a General Election, she climbed to the top of the Buckingham Town Hall with intent to erect the red flag. Eleanor fits into the long tradition of British eccentricity.' Stewart Graham, *The Spectator*

Someone's Been Done Up Harley
'In this book, Eleanor Berry's dazzling wit hits the Harley Street scene. Her extraordinary humour had me in stitches.' Thelma Masters, *The Oxford Times*

O, Hitman, My Hitman!
'Eleanor Berry's volatile pen is at it again. This time, she takes her readers back to the humorously eccentric Harley Street community. She also introduces Romany gypsies and travelling circuses, a trait which she has inherited from her self-confessed maternal gypsy aunt, the late writer, Eleanor Smith, after whom she was named. Like Smith, Berry is an inimitable and delightfully natural writer.' Kev Zein, *The Johannesburg Evening Sketch*

McArandy was Hanged on the Gibbet High
'We have here a potboiling, swashbuckling blockbuster, which is rich in adventure, intrigue, history, amorous episodes and black humour. The story Eleanor Berry tells is multi-coloured, multi-faceted and nothing short of fantastic.' Angel Z. Hogan, *The Daily Melbourne Times*

The Revenge of Miss Rhoda Buckleshott
'Words are Eleanor Berry's toys and her use of them is boundless.' Mary Hickman, professional historian and writer

The Most Singular Adventures of Eddy Vernon
'Rather a hot book for bedtime.' Nigel Dempster, *The Daily Mail*

Stop the Car, Mr Becket! (formerly *The Rendon Boy to the Grave is Gone*)
'This book makes for fascinating reading, as strange, black humoured and entertaining as Eleanor Berry's other books which came out before it.' Gaynor Evans, *The Bristol Evening Post*

Take it Away, It's Red!
'Despite the sometimes weighty portent of this book, a sense of subtle, dry and powerfully engaging humour reigns throughout its pages. The unexpected twist is stupendous.' Stephen Carson, *The Carolina Sun*

Sixty Funny Stories
'This book is a laugh a line.' Elisa Segrave, writer and diarist.

The House of the Weird Doctors
'This delightful medical caper puts even A.J. Cronin in the shade.' Noel I. Leskin, *The Stethoscope*

The Most Singular Adventures of Sarah Lloyd
'A riotous read from start to finish.' Ned McMurphy, *The Irish Times*

Alandra Varinia – Sarah's Daughter
'Eleanor Berry manages to maintain her raw and haunting wit as much as ever.' Dwight C. Farr, *The Texas Chronicle*

The Rise and Fall of Mad Silver Jaxton
'This time, Eleanor Berry tries her versatile hand at politics. Her sparkling wit and the reader's desire to turn the page are still in evidence. Eleanor Berry is unique.' Don F. Saunderson, *The South London Review*

'This is a dark, disturbing but at the same time hilarious tale of a megalomaniac dictator by the always readable and naughty Eleanor.' Sally Farmiloe, award-winning actress and author.

By the Fat of Unborn Leopards
'Could this ribald, grisly-humoured story about a British newspaper magnate's daughter, possibly be autobiographical, by any chance?' Peggy-Lou Kadinsky, *The Washington Globe*

'Fantastically black. A scream from beginning to end.' Charles Kidd, Editor of *Debrett's Peerage*

The Killing of Lucinda Maloney
'This is the funniest book I've read for months,' Samantha Morris, *The Exeter Daily News*

THE KILLING OF LUCINDA MALONEY

A humorous story of obsessive
compulsive disorder

Eleanor Berry
www.eleanorberry.net

Book Guild Publishing
Sussex, England

First published in Great Britain in 2012 by
The Book Guild Ltd
Pavilion View
19 New Road
Brighton, BN1 1UF

Typesetting in Baskerville by
Keyboard Services, Luton, Bedfordshire

Printed in Great Britain by
CPI Antony Rowe

A catalogue record for this book is available from
The British Library

ISBN 978 1 84624 741 5

For my brother, Adrian

The roads were treacherous. It was seven o'clock on a Friday evening in late January and it was snowing heavily. A married couple and their two babies were travelling to Cornwall in a second-hand Rover. The babies were twins, one of each sex.

The family were Londoners. Their destination was Launceston, in central Cornwall. They had never been there before, although the man's relatives had often visited the area. The couple had been asked to go there to settle a marital dispute between two old friends.

Their friends lived at the top of a steep tor or hill, near Launceston Castle. Many of the country lanes, leading to Launceston, were blocked by snowdrifts, piled up by north-easterly winds.

The small family reached a little hamlet near Launceston by about eight o'clock that night. The man was roughly twenty years old and the woman was eighteen years old. Like their prospective hosts, they too, had quarrelled. Neither of them had spoken since leaving London.

The woman was dark-haired and looked like a gypsy. The man had short, dark hair, parted at the side and Cary Grant looks. His wife was the first to break the silence.

'You're quite mad, getting us to come all this way, just to sort out the bloody Harveys' problems. They're not even our business,' she said.

'We've got to,' said the man. 'William and Jane have always been very nice to us. They're both a bit nutty, but we owe them a favour. It's not their fault that they're a

1

bit eccentric. Most people who live in the country are. Their brains ferment. They get weird.'

'We don't even know where their bloody house is,' said the woman. 'It would have helped if we'd left London earlier.'

'I couldn't take the afternoon off. William's given me directions. All we have to do is find the castle.'

They had reached the bottom of the steep tor, leading to the castle. There was a pause in their awkward conversation, broken by the woman.

'We need a four by four to get up there, not a bloody second-hand Rover. The children need changing and feeding. I'm the one who's got to do that, not you. You could have asked for the afternoon off. Not only that, Rovers have a sickly smell. The babies and I have been absolutely nauseated all the way here.'

The man wasn't listening to his wife. The Rover's wheels had become blocked by a four-foot snowdrift. He reversed a few feet, engaged first gear and revved up the engine. The Rover skidded on the road, and ended up facing the wrong way.

'Sorry,' said the man in an embarrassed tone. 'We'll have to go the rest of the way on foot.'

The blizzard's intensity had formed an icy snowdrift blocking the driver's side of the car. The woman unbelted the babies, lifted them from the back seat and dragged them out from the left side of the car. A heavy gust of wind blew against her, nearly knocking her and the babies over. The man scrambled over to the passenger's side, got out and took their suitcase out of the boot.

They started to walk up the tor in a stony silence, looking at the ground. The man slipped and fell over. He looked up and noticed the words Admiral Nelson Hotel, a few feet away from the road. Underneath, in small letters, nearly completely obscured by snow, he saw a sign, saying, 'All travellers welcome. Plenty of vacancies'.

The man called to his wife, who was trying to walk in her high-heeled shoes, ten feet behind him.

'There's a hotel here. It's got vacancies,' he said.

'I'd rather spend the night in a hotel than in the Harveys' house. We can ring them up on one of our mobile phones and tell them we won't be there until the morning,' said the woman.

The Admiral Nelson Hotel was two-star and was approached by a slippery driveway. The roof of the building was covered with blackened slates and the paint on the edges of the front door was chipped. The man rang the bell. Another man opened the door leading to the hall. There were no lights on in the hall, except for a naked bulb, hanging on a wire from the ceiling.

The hall was filthy and cold. There were piles of unwashed beer glasses and brimming ashtrays on the desk. A fat, unshaven, middle-aged man was sitting at the desk, leaning forward. He was the man who had opened the door. He was in his sixties but looked as if he were in his eighties. He had the bored, exhausted look of one whose life was dull, secluded and empty.

The visitor approached him, smiling.

'Have you got a room for me and my family, for one night?'

The hotelier's look changed. The expression on his face was like a sudden, glowing sun, lighting up a grey sky. His radiant smile suggested that he had not smiled for many months. His breath was foul and his teeth were blackened.

'That, I certainly have, sir!' He had a Cornish accent but gave the impression that he had not spoken for a long time. He waved his hand in the air as he spoke. His words were laboured, like a foreigner's.

3

'We 'ave rooms by the dozen. We don't often get visitors these days because it's winter-time. My wife and I get very lonely. We lead separate lives. We don't get on too well so we haven't even got each other. It seems to be the case all the year round but the winters are worse. It's meant a lot to me to meet you, sir. Loneliness can destroy anyone. The fact that you've come here with your family has brought out the sunshine in my heart. I'll just go through the formalities, like taking your names. My wife noticed you coming in and she's lit a gas-fire in the bar for you all.'

'That's very kind of you indeed,' said the man. The hotelier's strong Cornish accent had made him feel self-conscious. He inadvertently allowed his upper-class accent to become more pronounced.

'Where are you from, sir?' asked the Cornishman.

'London.'

The Cornishman felt humbled. To him, London sounded like Mars. The intrusion of a Londoner into a part of the country he had lived in all his life angered and belittled him, but his finances and desolation forced him to be friendly.

'So 'tis London you've come from, is it? That's a long, long way from here. I've never been there in all my blessed days.'

'Oh, indeed?'

' 'Tis a shame, isn't it? I don't think I want to go there, though. They say 'tis a wicked place, a den of iniquity, a terrible, terrible place...' He sounded like a desperado, calling for plague victims to be brought from their houses and thrown into death carts.

'I can assure you, it's not like that at all,' said the Londoner, whose wife sat on a broken wicker chair in the corner of the hall. She had begun to feed her twin babies from each breast. As she did so, she rocked backwards and forwards, loudly singing *Early One Morning*, to make her frustration more apparent to the Cornishman, and to show her anger towards him, for having cast aspersions on the city in which she had been born and raised.

The Cornishman suddenly extended his hand to the Londoner. 'I never meant to insult you, sir. You be a gentleman, if ever there was one. Here's my dusty, old visitors' book. 'Tis an honour to have you all here. You're our first visitors since last May. Could I be troubling you for your names? I should have told you, I'm Jack Menhenniot.'

'How do you do, Mr Menhenniot. My name is Arthur Flinton. This lady is my wife, Judith Flinton and our twin babies are called John and Jennifer Flinton.'

It was then that something unnerving happened. Menhenniot stared Arthur in the eye, with an expression of chilling, calculated evil. Arthur looked away. Menhenniot's change from warmth to hatred puzzled him.

'Is there something the matter?' he asked.

Menhenniot sprawled over the desk. His and Arthur's faces were almost touching. Their profiles looked like those of the two characters towards the end of the famous film, *The Odd Couple*. Menhenniot grabbed his visitor by the collar.

'Are you in any way related to *Joshua* Flinton?' The question was a combination of a hiss and a shout.

'Flinton's a very common name,' said Arthur guardedly. He added, 'There are dozens of them about. If someone called Flinton has offended you in some way, I'm sure he is no relation of mine. I had an uncle by that name though. I've got a photograph of him in my pocket.'

'Is your uncle called Joshua Flinton?' asked Menhenniot. By now, he was in a savage rage.

Arthur evaded the question. He took a frayed photograph out of his pocket and passed it to Menhenniot.

'That's my uncle. He's the one in the middle. The photograph was taken on our wedding day.'

Menhenniot held the photograph up to the light. A dark haired, good-looking man (Joshua) was standing between the bride and groom. Menhenniot was struck by the likeness the dark-haired man bore to the groom.

He slapped the photograph on the desk in a demented bait.

'Get your bloody arse out of here, and your fucking family, as well!' he bellowed.

'How dare you use that filthy, disgusting language in front of my wife!' shouted Arthur. 'You've frightened the babies and made them cry. Is there a history of insanity in your family?'

Menhenniot left the desk and paced nervously up and down the tiny hall like an expectant father.

'So you're Joshua Flinton's nephew,' he said, this time more quietly. Mrs Menhenniot came from the bar into the hall. She looked as if she were in her late seventies. Her sluttish appearance was intimidating. Her small, piercing black eyes were out of focus. Her skin was deeply lined. She gave the Flintons a sinister, reluctant smile, showing a single front tooth.

'What's wrong, Jack?' she asked Menhenniot.

'This fellow's related to Joshua Flinton,' said her husband, 'the basket case we had in here last May, the writer, the maniac in room sixteen. This man is his bloody nephew, Arthur Flinton. Joshua Flinton got in his cups one night and said he was trying to finish a book called *The Killing of Lucinda Maloney*. Don't you remember?'

'Aye, I remember,' said Mrs Menhenniot in a surly tone.

Arthur decided he would resist if Menhenniot tried to force him and his family to leave the hotel. The car was covered with snow and ice and was short of petrol. If the family tried to sleep in it, he knew they would not survive. He followed Menhenniot into the bar.

'You asked me just now if I was related to Joshua Flinton.

6

Yes, I was. He was my uncle, as I said earlier. I know he occasionally had funny turns.'

Menhenniot was baffled. 'Why are you using the past tense?' he asked suspiciously.

'Because no one knows where he is. No one's seen or heard of him for at least eight months. He was a kind, sweet-natured person. What did he do to make you so angry?'

Menhenniot let out a smoker's cough and an expiry of foul breath. Arthur jumped backwards and covered his mouth to hold his bile.

'He seemed all right during the day. It was the things he did one night that were so fearsome. The man was a psychopath,' said Menhenniot. He let out a rattling smoker's cough once more. He continued, 'He said he was writing the book I mentioned which appeared to be upsetting him. He went on and on about having to kill the heroine off, because she was too much for him to bear.'

Arthur was puzzled by Menhenniot's sudden articulate use of words. He said, 'If my uncle said that, he must have known you quite well. A writer doesn't say that sort of thing unless he really trusts the person he's speaking to. It sounds as if he'd been here *before* his visit last May. Had he?'

'No, he only came here once. He got badly in his cups one night and blurted out his problems, as I said.' Menhenniot coughed again. He continued, 'He came here last May, as I told you just now. He drove my wife, myself and everyone staying in this hotel, off their heads. I've now got cirrhosis of the liver because of him.'

'What, exactly did he do, when he came here last May? When you're telling me, keep your voice down and your story brief. You're frightening the babies again.'

Menhenniot sat on the rotating chair behind the desk in the hall.

'I suppose you'd better bring your wife and family into the bar,' he said. 'My wife will tell you what your uncle did. I haven't got the stomach for it.'

'He didn't murder anyone, did he?' asked Joshua.

'No. If he had, it wouldn't have been any worse than what he did. When my wife's finished telling you, I want the whole bloody lot of you out.'

'Not in these weather conditions, mister!' said Arthur, adding, 'we're nearly out of petrol and we wouldn't survive the night.'

Menhenniot was frightened of Arthur, whom he feared might have inherited his uncle's genes. He showed the Flinton family into the bar. His wife followed them, shuffling like an exhausted, slatternly drunk.

The carpet in the bar was unhoovered and like the hall the bar was covered with dust and unemptied ashtrays. The only cheerful feature was a gas fire.

Menhenniot went behind the bar and poured himself some neat whisky. He then poured some for his wife who sat grotesquely on a bar stool with her legs wide apart.

'Want anything to drink, Flinton?' asked Menhenniot abruptly.

'I'll have a double whisky and soda. My wife will have a gin and tonic. It wouldn't go amiss if you addressed me as "Mr Flinton", instead of just "Flinton".'

Menhenniot poured out more whisky and drained his glass, after which he poured out whisky and soda for Joshua and gin and tonic for his wife. Then he leant across the bar and prodded his wife in the ribs, like a farmer poking an ageing sow.

'OK, maid, spill the story about this man's bloody uncle, and his terrifying behaviour that night last May,' he said, adding, 'I'm going to bed and I'll leave my wife alone with you. When you go up, you'll be sleeping in room sixteen, the room in which your uncle disgraced himself! You'll only be staying for one night, no longer.'

'Thank you,' said Arthur. 'I don't want feelings between us to get even worse than they are already. How much do we owe you for the night?'

Menhenniot scrutinized the elegant clothes worn by the parents of the babies and assumed that the Flintons were wealthy.

'I'll take two hundred and fifty pounds,' he said in a surly tone.

Arthur opened his leather, monogrammed wallet in which he kept his cheque book. He wrote out a cheque for two hundred and fifty pounds and passed it to Menhenniot who snatched it from his hand.

'Just before we go to bed, I'd like to tell you something,' said Arthur.

'Yes?'

'The Flintons are a very big family. I'll tell all my relatives about your nice, clean, comfortable hotel and your extreme hospitality and I'll send them down here in droves.'

Mrs Menhenniot continued to sit on the bar stool. She then told Arthur exactly what his uncle had done in room sixteen. And a most singular story it was too.

Joshua David Flinton came from a wealthy family. He was the youngest of two boys. He had thick, black hair, a full face and brown eyes. He had a brother called Charles Nicholas Flinton who was five years his senior. Their mother had left her husband for another man. The children were too young to remember her well although Charles remembered her slightly.

Their father, Edward John Flinton, had been an Oxford don and had inherited a large, unearned income from his father and grandfather. He looked quite like Joshua but

9

had lighter hair and a thinner face. He had met his wife, Suzie, when she was an undergraduate attending one of his lectures. He found her attractive but she became bored, foul-tempered and promiscuous after Joshua was born. She also suffered from post-natal depression.

Edward was relieved when she left him. He was an intense, quiet man who hated hysterical women when they shouted and threw crockery about. He was an antisocial recluse. His sister, Rita, a concert pianist to whom he was very close, was two years older than he was. She was his only sibling. She and Edward were born and bred in a large house on Hampstead Heath, London.

Edward had been a controversial don in Russian literature at Balliol College, Oxford. He was a difficult man to get on with because of his refusal to mix with his colleagues. His relations with other dons in his faculty were poor. They considered him to be a bore who suffered from obsessive compulsive disorder.

They were also irritated by what they referred to as his 'pompous, eccentric lecturing methods'. They considered his choice of words when talking to bemused undergraduates childish, stilted and devoid of scholarship.

An incident was blown out of proportion, halfway through one of Edward's particularly bizarre lectures. There was a stifling heatwave. The hot tempers of dons and under-graduates alike soared. Edward was even more intolerant of the heat than his colleagues. He was due to give a lecture on nineteenth-century Russian literature. The lecture was the worst he had given in his entire career.

The animosity of the other dons towards him had reached a peak and they began to torment him, hoping that their backbiting would drive him away from the university. A campaign to bring Edward to his knees was embarked upon by a certain Professor Black who had been an electrician in his student days. Black wired the lecture hall which Edward would be using so that the dons could play a recording of his words in crowded places and humiliate him.

That day, Edward started speaking without preamble. His greatest disadvantages were his monotonous voice and his failure to command the respect of the undergraduates listening to his deliberations.

'I took up the study of nineteenth-century Russian literature in my early teens,' he began. 'I don't know whether anyone in this room has at any time been traumatized by its prevailing, moribund tones and its somewhat fatalistic undercurrent.' He cleared his throat nervously.

A shuffling sound, accompanied by yawning noises, greeted his words. He continued, 'If anyone wishes to comment on psychological trauma associated with Russian literature during that period, would they please raise their hand. That way, a meaty and hopefully stimulating discussion can be initiated.'

No one raised their hand. Some of the undergraduates had fallen asleep. Edward continued, 'Although the weather is unusually hot, I do feel this most fascinating matter, *vis-à-vis* the traumatic effects that many nineteen-century Russian writers can have on the reader, has simply *got* to be addressed, courageously and robustly. Is there no one in the room with an opinion about this matter?'

A girl with large breasts, long, straight chestnut-coloured hair and a beautiful nose, raised her hand. Edward felt as if he had been offered a bottle of water in a desert.

'Ah, yes, young lady. May I hear your views about morbidity in nineteenth-century Russian literature?'

'I only put my hand up because of the heat, not to talk about whether I've been traumatised by nineteenth-century Russian literature. All I wanted was to ask you if you could open the windows,' said the girl rather rudely.

'Windows? Windows? Why, yes, I suppose I can. Weather reporters are saying that temperatures have risen to ninety degrees Fahrenheit in the shade this week. What we need is a downpour.' He added, 'I say, these windows seem pretty stiff, could you try opening them yourself? Throw your whole weight on the ropes. That should get them open.'

The girl did so without much difficulty. When she had done so, she went back to her seat.

'Well, young lady?' said Edward.

'I don't think morbidity plays a particularly significant part in nineteenth-century Russian literature,' the girl said.

'What about the poetical works of Pushkin?' asked Edward.

'What about them?'

'What can you tell us about his treatment of morbidity and melancholic themes?'

'I don't think his stuff is particularly morbid or melancholy, except the poem he wrote about his nanny's death. His poem, *Tsar Nikita and his Forty Daughters* is meant to be humorous.'

'I'm a bit surprised that you find it comical if girls are born without vaginas,' said Edward assertively.

'Pushkin obviously thought it was comical,' said the girl.

'Could we return to the issue concerning morbidity, as opposed to ribaldry?'

'I think you've got a one-track mind, sir. I've found little morbidity in Russian literature in the nineteenth century, as I said a few moments ago,' repeated the girl.

'Could I refer you to *Crime and Punishment*?' said Edward. 'How do you feel about its authorial presentation?'

'That book's not morbid. It's an attractive and optimistic book. Despite the earlier part of the book, which is a bit turgid, I admit, Sonia and Rodion Romanovich get together eventually. It's implied that they do so once he gets out of prison. Also, the book is extremely droll in places. I refer to the scene at the police station. I agree that that Marmeladov fellow bangs on as if someone had put Dexedrine in his vodka. You're obviously obsessed by death. You should be a funeral director, not a don.'

Edward had a contrived coughing fit.

'Through your familiarity with the works of Gogol, this time, have you noticed any tones, however minor, of subconscious necrophilia in his prose, or any other signs of sad psychological trends?'

'Jesus, sir, you're possessed! Are you seeing a specialist?' ventured the girl in an insolent tone.

'This does not call for impertinence. Have you cited any necrophile preoccupation in any of Gogol's works?'

'No, of course, I haven't. The fella just wasn't into stiffs.'

'Have you neglected his *Taras Bulba*? When you answer, would you please avoid the use of slang words.'

'I haven't neglected the blasted book,' said the girl, adding, 'I've read it twice and I've seen the film once. Tony Curtis, as Andrei, was a right barrel of laughs.' The girl added, in order to show off, 'I understand that the first edition of the book, was entitled *Lyubov Andrei*.'*

'I'm afraid you haven't read the book carefully enough. We are towards the end when Taras, a Cossack, shoots his son Andrei dead because he defected to the Polish armies through love of a Polish woman. Gogol uses the following language. "Andrei fell like an ear of corn, cut down by the sickle. How supremely beautiful he looked in death"!'

'So what, sir? That's got nothing to do with necrophilia.

* *Lyubov Andrei: Andrei's Love.*

13

It just states that the bloke looked beautiful. I don't mean to be rude but I feel that much of your vision of nineteenth-century Russian literature is critically distorted. You only look at it from one angle. You have turned an ennobling and glorious thing into something unwholesome. Your attitude towards it is ghoulish. You shouldn't have chosen to be a don in Russian literature. You should spend your time writing about carrion birds hovering over corpses!'

'I don't think this discussion calls for rudeness, young lady. It's started to pour with rain, blast it! Would you please go and close all the windows you opened.'

Some of the undergraduates giggled. Edward paced up and down nervously, before speaking again. He spoke to the same girl.

'I feel we should move on, and address what should be recognized as morbid and bleak themes in nineteenth century Russian literature in a serious manner. These are often found in the works of the Steppe glorification lads who bask in desolation and despair. Define a "Steppe glorification lad", would you please, young lady, and comment on it.'

'It means a dickhead who rabbits on and on about the alleged beauty of the Steppes,' said the same girl, adding rudely, 'I don't think they're beautiful at all. They look like a fucking rent boy's tits.'

'You still haven't closed those windows,' said Edward, who was too shocked at first to comment on the girl's language.

'What do you want me to do first, sir – comment on the desolation and despair flowing from the pens of what you refer to as the "Steppe glorification lads", or close the bloody windows?'

'Use your common sense. Close the windows first. Then sit down and offer your comments in a civil manner, this time avoiding the use of filthy, disgusting language.'

'It would save time if I offered my comments and closed the windows at the same time, sir.'

Edward was intimidated but attracted by the girl's cheekiness. At the end of the lecture he followed her to the door.

'What's your name?' he asked.

'Suzie Jones.'

'Are you free this evening?'

'No. I'm going out,' said Suzie, without looking Edward in the eye.

'What about tomorrow night?'

'I'm free then.'

'You did say your name was Suzie Jones, didn't you?'

'That's right. I've just said so.'

'You are known to most of the dons at this college.'

'Why?'

'Because of that essay you wrote about Nietzsche. You headed your essay, "On the Taboo against Ego-Tripping". You're doing a contextual course in philosophy, are you not?'

'Yes. What about it?'

'You wrote the most extraordinary essay about a month ago. One of the dons photocopied it and put it on the staff notice board.'

'I know the essay you're referring to. What was so extraordinary about it?' asked Suzie.

'Your staccato, peremptory prose, for one thing, like your speech. You baffled everyone by the words with which you started your essay: "Jesus, Nietzsche, if you'll pardon my neat little juxtaposition".'

'What's wrong with that?' asked Suzie.

'It was so cheeky. It showed both shallowness and daring. I get the impression that you think nothing of doing things others wouldn't dare to do.'

'Perhaps that's true. I like to be seen on a pedestal

above others. I've always been an exhibitionist,' confessed Suzie with a conspiratorial smile.

Edward was entranced by Suzie. She reminded him of a fresh, apple-cheeked American high-school girl, a 'tennis anyone?' type, the type of person who drank cold milk with all her meals.

'Before I meet you for dinner tomorrow night, I'll have to bone up a bit about morbid elements in the works of the "Steppe glorification lads",' said Suzie in a sneering tone.

'Why did you say that?'

'In case that's the only bloody subject you want to talk to me about.'

'I can assure you it isn't.'

'Is that guaranteed?'

'Everything I say is guaranteed.'

Professor Black and three other dons specializing in Russian literature were in the men's lavatory. They had been listening to Flinton's lecture, which Black had bugged and which had come through into the headphones they were wearing as they stood facing the urinals.

Professor Black was in a state of mischievous glee and was laughing secretively.

'What's started you off, Blackie? Have you found the perfect muse for those ponderous verses of yours?' asked one of the dons.

'I'm listening to the bugged lecture Flinton's just given. It's hardly what you'd call academic. Anyone who refers to Russian writers as "Steppe glorification lads" needs to see a highly qualified, first-class psychiatrist. There's no place for the old fool here.'

Professor Black and the three other dons were startled when Edward came into the lavatory. He had heard them talking about him as he walked down the corridor. The dons turned round, looked at him and fixed him with underhand smiles.

Edward lowered his head with embarrassment, went into a cubicle and locked the door.

The dons, who might just as well have been ten-year-old playground bullies, gathered outside the door of Flinton's cubicle and sang a song to the tune of *Men of Harlech*.

> *'Flinton, Flinton, Delta Minus,*
> *Flinton, Flinton, Delta Minus...'*

Later, Professor Black played the song and the bugged lecture from loudspeakers in Balliol College's quadrangle.

Edward knew he was clever but he realized the game was up for him. He left Oxford, settled in north London in a large Queen Anne house, became a reclusive man of letters and began to write a lengthy biography of Gavriil Derzhavin, a late eighteenth-century Russian poet. He married Suzie Jones who only agreed to marry him because of his wealth. He spent every day and evening writing. Suzie regretted marrying him as he never went out in the evenings.

She gave birth to two sons, the eldest of whom was called Charles Nicholas. At that period of his life, Edward continued to be obsessively bitter about the way the other Oxford dons had treated him. As they were not there for him to take revenge on them, he used Charles as a scapegoat, knowing that he could not return the insults and injuries which had been inflicted on him.

Sometimes, when Charles was sitting on the floor, playing with his bricks, Edward kicked the bricks over and occasionally kicked him in the behind.

Joshua, Edward's youngest son, was born when Charles was five years old. Edward was then in his twenties. Suzie suffered from post-natal depression after Joshua's birth. She continuously berated Edward about his treatment of Charles. She was violent, threw crockery about and slept around. This went on for some time. Her condition was recalcitrant and was even described by a top Harley Street psychiatrist as being 'malignant'. She was committed to a fancy mental institution at her husband's expense and when she finally recovered she went off with another man.

Edward had become besotted by his six-month-old son, Joshua. His father's love was strengthened dramatically when Joshua caught septicaemia and was rushed to Great Ormond Street Hospital for Sick Children in London.

Edward stayed in the hospital and was terrified of falling asleep in case Joshua died without him witnessing his death. He resented the fact that his eldest son, Charles, was healthy and chubby, while his favourite son lay in an incubator hovering between life and death.

Joshua was not recovering; he was deteriorating. Edward despaired of his recovery. He found out who his local parson was and wept on the phone as he discussed funeral arrangements.

He went back to Great Ormond Street Hospital and came to the ward where Joshua was incarcerated. A nurse ran towards him. He assumed she had come to tell him that Joshua had died. He wondered why she was smiling.

'It's good news, sir,' she said. 'Joshua's temperature is down. He's reacting to the antibiotics. The consultant, Dr Greenwood, examined him when you were out. He assured us that he has turned the corner. That means he's going to live. We will have to do a series of scans as a formality, though.'

'Why?' asked Edward suspiciously.

'To make sure that there is nothing wrong with any of his vital organs.'

'When will you know the results of the scans?'

'In the case of an in-patient, within twenty-four hours.

We should know the results by the time you come to see him tomorrow morning.'

Edward went to the hospital the following morning. He was told by a nurse that an SHO* would be coming to speak to him.

'How much longer will I have to wait?' asked Edward impatiently.

'Not long, Mr Flinton. Dr Farr, the SHO to Dr Greenwood, has said he will be coming up to have a word with you shortly,' said the nurse.

'Why have I got to see a bloody SHO? I'd rather see a consultant,' said Edward.

'I'm afraid the consultant on Joshua's case is lecturing at the moment. I'll get some tea brought in for you.'

Dr Farr came into the room fifteen minutes later.

'I'm sorry to have kept you waiting for so long, Mr Flinton,' he said, adding, 'We have done scans of all Joshua's vital organs and almost all of them are normal. However, there is one marked abnormality, and that is in the brain. I'll go through the MRI scan of Joshua's brain with you. It won't take more than a few minutes.'

Dr Farr slapped the MRI scan of Joshua's brain onto an illuminated screen attached to the wall.

'That's all very well but I've got no idea what any of this means,' said Edward peremptorily. He added: 'How badly affected is my son's brain?'

Dr Farr cleared his throat. 'The defect is not very pronounced on the MRI scan but there is a significant abnormality and evidence that your son will be mentally deranged when he gets older,' said Dr Farr, adding, 'It's quite possible that neither he nor those close to him will notice anything wrong at first. He may well be able to

*Senior house officer: euphemism for a junior doctor.

19

live a productive, normal, early life, but there is an indication that he will develop a damaged personality, which will become worse as he gets older.'

'When?' asked Edward.

'My colleagues and I feel it will be unlikely that there will be signs of mental abnormality until Joshua's late teens, or maybe even his early adulthood.'

'If that happens, how serious will it be?' asked Edward.

'Joshua will appear normal most of the time during his adolescence but there will still be episodes of mental disorder, as I said. The episodes may not start until he is in his twenties. They will be slight at first but will eventually turn to what in layman's terms constitutes full-blown insanity. He is likely to suffer from epilepsy as well. On the credit side, he may be extremely clever before he loses his mind.'

'Oh, holy mother!' muttered Edward.

Charles was fifteen years old and Joshua was ten years old. Charles looked more like his father than Joshua did. His hair was light and his face was gaunt. All three had sad brown eyes. Edward realized that Joshua, young as he was, had inherited his gift for writing although he was only ten years old. Edward admired his youngest son's doggedness and loved him more than Charles because of his frailty and vulnerability.

At about that time, Edward, Charles and Joshua spent their summer holidays writing. They sat on the terrace of their house at a marble table, overlooking a lawn. Edward preferred to write with an old war-time typewriter but he had given Charles a word processor (a birthday present). Joshua preferred to write by hand.

Edward continued to write his long biography of Gavriil Derzhavin. Charles was very keen on Ian Fleming's novels and wrote enterprising, intriguing but nonsensical books about espionage. One of his books was sixty thousand words long. It was entitled *The Palestinian Pilots and the Chewing Gum.*

'What's the title of your book, Charles?' asked Edward. Charles told him.

'That's a bloody stupid title!'

'Maybe, you're right. The main characters are Palestinian helicopter pilots who are on an espionage mission.'

'Where do they land?' asked Edward.

'In an Israeli cemetery,' replied his son, who had no intelligent answer ready.

'Why do they land there? That's plain silly,' said Edward irritably.

'Perhaps I could get them to land in a field about a mile away from the cemetery. When they've landed, the helicopter, whose pilot and co-pilot are armed with grenades, seek out two Israeli soldiers. One of the Palestinian pilots has got a fantastic Al-Capone-style *Mashi.*'

'Do you mean a machine gun?' asked Edward angrily. 'Yes.'

'Then say so, for God's sake! You don't give any thought at all to your work. Go on.'

'The Palestinian pilot and co-pilot are so tired that they go back to their helicopter and fall asleep. The Israeli soldiers get strips of chewing gum from their pockets, chew them to make them sticky and block the Palestinian helicopter's engine with them, while the pilot and co-pilot are asleep.'

'How do the Israeli soldiers gain access to the engine of the Palestinians' helicopter?' asked Edward.

'I haven't worked that out yet. They just do.'

'It sounds as if your book's a non-starter, like the Palestinian pilots. It's infantile. Why don't you try something else? Yours is the work of a seven-year-old, not a boy of your age.'

Charles was humiliated. 'All right, Daddy. I'll start another book,' he muttered.

The writing routine during the summer holidays continued for some years. Charles was twenty years old and unemployed. Joshua was fifteen years old and was still at school. He attended the Westminster School for Boys where his brother had been educated. Edward had had published his biography of Gavriil Derzhavin and was writing a new book, a biography of Vasily Zhukovsky, another late eighteenth-century Russian poet.

Joshua was noisy and precocious. Edward was relieved to see that there appeared to be nothing wrong, either with his personality or his intellect at the time.

Edward spoiled and pampered Joshua whom he treated like a porcelain ornament. Like his father, the younger boy had continued to show a rare talent for writing. Charles remained glued to espionage and still imitated the style and themes of Ian Fleming.

Joshua's writing was outrageous but enterprising. His themes were ribald, grisly and macabre. They were perversely disturbing and occasionally pornographic. He specialized in gallows humour. Edward did not overtly encourage or condone the subjects his youngest son wrote about but was strangely entranced by them. Charles was excluded from the bond, linking his father with his younger brother.

Edward did not mind Joshua's themes, which were warped and sometimes profoundly embarrassing. He was extremely critical of Charles's work, in comparison with the doting attitude which he showed towards anything Joshua wrote.

The father and his two sons were having lunch at the marble table which the three used for eating as well as writing. A butler was passing trays of cottage pie from one to the other, first to Edward, then to Charles and finally to Joshua. Edward turned to face Charles.

'I'm getting a bit fed up with the monotony of your work, Charles. You have admitted that you emulate Ian Fleming but you don't read the works of any other authors. Your scope is limited, your prose is awkward and your plots are repetitive and adolescent. Your characters are wooden, with neither light nor shade. Overall, you're an awful bore.'

Charles was upset by his father's words.

'In what way am I an awful bore?' he asked, in a humiliated tone.

'Your sentence structure has a jarring effect on the reader. Its identification with Ian Fleming's style is irritating and tedious. I can remember a sentence from his prose, and another from yours. In one of his books, he says: "Bond said: 'Load my Smith & Wesson, would you, old boy?'" Instead, Fleming should have written: "'Load my Smith & Wesson, would you, old boy?" said Bond.' In the book you're writing at the moment, you have said, "Colonel Jackson said: 'Give me two pounds to tip my driver.'" Your sentence should have been structured the other way round but you deliberately reversed your words out of affectation.'

'Have you got anything complimentary to say about my work?' asked Charles sadly, his eyes dewy.

'How can I have? You told me you were thinking of offering your manuscripts to Lord Brook-Owen. He's the most prestigious publisher in London. What gives you the impression that any readers on his firm will find your work acceptable in this condition?'

Charles was furious with his father but was too timid to get into an argument with him.

'I'm going to make a lot of alterations, of course,' he whispered.

There was a silence of about five minutes, which was broken by Charles.

'Joshua, pass the mustard.'

'Pass the mustard, *what*?' said Joshua.

Edward was amused and delighted by his youngest son's rebellious behaviour and laughed. For a short time, Joshua was pleased to have been able to make his father laugh and to exclude his brother from his relationship with the older man.

'Come on, Joshua, *please* pass the mustard,' said Charles.

Joshua laughed to himself and looked conspiratorially at his father. An outsider might have found the bond between the two extremely creepy. Joshua passed the pepper to Charles.

The atmosphere at the table became even more unpleasant.

'Could you pass me the bread, please,' said Joshua. Charles offered him a jug of water. Edward looked bored and angry.

'Stop being so bloody childish, Charles. Give him the bread when he asks for it and don't torment the poor little chap, who is five years your junior but writes as if he were five years your senior.'

Incidents of this nature gradually alienated one brother from the other even more. The father and the younger brother continued to be united by a weird bond, excluding Charles.

The three were having dinner.

'How's that naughty book of yours coming along, Joshua, old fellow?' asked Edward affectionately.

'It's OK. I'm up to the point where John and Jackie rush urgently into a barn to consummate their lust,' said Joshua. He put his hand over his mouth and let out a coy laugh.

'This is what I've written, Daddy,' he said proudly: '"Jackie suddenly realized that she had forgotten to put in her cap. 'Don't worry,' said John, 'we'll do things differently. I haven't brought my jar of Vaseline with me just fo the hell of it.'" Saucy, eh?' he said. 'And a bit ribald as well.'

'Your literary style is coming along very well for a boy of your age. Although you're a bit wicked, you're showing a lot of promise. You'll be a best-selling writer one day; I know it in my bones.'

'What about me?' asked Charles.

Edward wiped his mouth with his napkin, which he put on his knee after using it.

'I rather think not, Charles,' he said coldly.

Charles found breakfasts even more unpleasant than lunches, teas and dinners.

Joshua had woken Charles up by blaring a transistor radio in the room which the two brothers shared. Their father had given it to him for his birthday. The elder brother had retaliated by picking the radio up and throwing it against a wall, smashing it.

Joshua came to the breakfast table in tears.

'What's the matter, old fellow?' asked Edward sympathetically.

'Nothing,' said Joshua.

'There must be *something* the matter.'

Joshua poured milk and sugar onto his cornflakes.

'I'm sure there is. You're just afraid to tell me, aren't you?' said Edward.

Joshua still refused to answer. Edward fixed Charles with a penetrating, suspicious stare.

'What did you do to him, Charles?'

'I didn't do anything. Why do I always have to get the blame?'

'Because you fail to give satisfaction all round. Just before I went to sleep last night, I continued to read your new manuscript. Your book is set in East Berlin in

1965. You describe the escape of a family from East Berlin to the West.

'Your work is childish. One of your characters is an East German postman, bearing the ludicrous name of Andy Slapstick. It's clear that you've run out of ideas so you go on and on about Herr Slapstick's blasted bathroom. You say the walls of his bathroom are covered with Van Dykes and that the bath itself is sunken and filled with asses' milk,' said Edward, adding, 'How on earth do you think a postman living in East Berlin in 1965 could have afforded to bathe in a sunken bath filled with asses' milk?'

'You must have misread what I wrote,' said Charles who was close to tears. 'This family are rich West Berliners, moving to the East. Herr Slapstick is guilty about his inherited wealth and, in particular, about his family's ornate, ostentatious bathroom.'

'I see,' said Edward. 'You certainly haven't explained yourself very clearly. The whole book is unworthy of a boy of your age. A much younger boy than you would know better than to tell a story like that. What do you think, Joshua, or have you not read Charles's manuscript yet?'

'I'm afraid I haven't read it so I can't comment on it,' said Joshua guardedly.

'I'm sure you have but you don't dare say anything, in case Charles beats you when I'm not here.'

The butler came onto the terrace and said Edward was wanted on the phone. Charles and Joshua sat awkwardly with their heads lowered.

'You'll never be a writer. Your ideas aren't nearly as intelligent as mine,' said Charles, adding, 'Your books are too morbid and pornographic.'

'That's not a very nice thing to say. I covered up for you about the radio, didn't I?' said Joshua.

'You'd only cover up for me by making yourself permanently absent,' said Charles.

'Why did you say that? I covered up for you about the radio, didn't I?' repeated Joshua.

'You'd only cover up for me by making yourself permanently absent, as I've just said,' said Charles once more.

'Do you think I enjoy it, when you two do nothing but quarrel?'

'Yes. I think you enjoy every minute of it,' replied Charles, adding, 'The only reason you're Daddy's favourite, is that a typed report of an MRI scan done of your brain, which I found in one of his drawers, showed your brain when you were a baby at Great Ormond Street Hospital for Sick Children in London. I read the report accompanying the MRI scan. It said that your brain is damaged and that the damage will get worse as you get older. In fact, the report said you'll probably end up by becoming completely insane. You had septicaemia when you were a baby. It was that which affected your brain. The report also said you'd be likely to become epileptic.'

'What MRI scan? When was it done?' asked Joshua.

'Of course, you were never told. You were only a few months old,' said Charles. 'The whole thing was hushed up. It's been proved there's something wrong with your brain. You don't know anything about it yet but as you get older, you'll go madder and madder.'

'I do wish you'd leave me alone, Charles,' said Joshua mildly.

Another unpleasant incident occurred a few days later. The family were sitting, writing. Edward was using his old-fashioned typewriter. Charles was using his word processor and Joshua was writing by hand.

Suddenly, Charles got up and forced a feather quill pen into his brother's hand.

'What did you do that for, Charles?' asked Joshua.

'Because if you're to become a professional writer, you'll have to adjust to modern technology.'

'I prefer writing by hand.'

Edward was sitting at his noisy, rattling typewriter, working on his biography of Vasily Zhukovsky, but was alerted by the argument between his sons.

'Will you leave that boy alone!' he shouted to Charles.

'I was only trying to help him. You offered to buy him a word processor but he turned your offer down. I told him he will never become a professional writer unless he uses one.'

'Joshua's writing skills are much more imaginative and original than yours. He's got a fine mind. Also, he likes to write everything down in his nice, neat, tidy handwriting, don't you, my boy?' said Edward.

Edward went to see his publisher the following day. His publisher had long since published his book about Derzhavin. Charles and Joshua were left alone at the lunch table.

'I resent the way you get all the praise and me the blame,' said the elder brother.

'It's not as if I encourage it.'

'You do, to a very great extent. The two of you are always ganging up against me. It's quite sinister, the way you carry on.'

'I certainly don't. All I want is a quiet life.'

'That's a lie. You don't often use words. You gain Daddy's approval by making gestures. I'm referring to the shifty way you smile at him whenever he ticks me off.'

'That's not true. All I want is for us both to be friends,' said Joshua, adding, 'I can't stand these arguments.'

Charles, then twenty-five years old, had been attracted to an eighteen-year-old girl. Her name was Isabel Sikes, and she was Edward's gardener's daughter. She had married a man six years her senior a few months before.

She had arranged to meet Charles in a shed at the

bottom of the garden. The pair were lying on the floor in the shed, having noisy sex.

Edward happened to be walking in the garden, hoping to find the gardener whom he wanted to talk to about the planting of some bulbs. As he approached the shed near the flower bed where the bulbs were to be planted, he heard loud laughter. He went in and found his son lying naked on top of his employee's daughter.

'I'd like a word with you back at the house, Charles, in the library,' he said sternly.

Charles sat down in front of the large leather-topped desk in the library. Edward sat on the other side of it. His son was intimidated by the austere atmosphere in the room, even though he had long since come of age.

'Did you know that Isabel, the gardener's daughter, got married a few months ago?' asked Edward.

'I didn't know. I had an idea she was single.'

'You know that's a lie. This is not the kind of behaviour that one would expect from a boy of twenty-five. It certainly isn't the sort of thing a decent boy like Joshua would do.'

'All I can say is "sorry", said Charles. 'Is there anything else you want to speak to me about?'

'Yes, there is. It relates to behaviour even worse than the other matter.'

'What behaviour?'

'Joshua asked me yesterday whether he had had an MRI scan of his brain done at Great Ormond Street Hospital for Sick Children when he was a baby. He also asked me if it showed that he would gradually become insane in later years. You and I were the only people who knew about the MRI scan and what it entailed. I did not tell Joshua about it for obvious reasons. Only one other person knew. That person was you. You told him, didn't you?'

Charles was embarrassed and rocked backwards and forwards in his chair. He decided to lie to his father once more.

'I didn't tell him. He told me he'd visited the hospital where the MRI scan had taken place in his infancy. He did so because he's been suffering from headaches of late. That's what he told me.'

'How would he have known that he'd been in that particular hospital when he was a baby?' asked Edward.

'It's possible he'd been rummaging through your drawers and that he found the medical report. He does that sometimes. He told me so.'

Edward flew into a towering rage and banged his fist on the desk.

'You lie! You lie! You lie! You lie! You told him because you wanted to upset him. You're a shit, Charles, and because you are dishonest, unlike Joshua and me, I suspect you may not be my son. You're probably the product of one of your mother's murky love affairs. An elder brother is supposed to be good-natured towards a boy five years his junior, as I have continuously pointed out to you over the years.' Edward added, 'You've been cruel to Joshua every time I've seen you together.'

'I don't really think that's fair,' ventured Charles.

'Oh, you don't, do you? It's time you took justice from me,' shouted Edward at the top of his voice, adding, 'I'm leaving you nothing in my will. Everything I own is going to Joshua. You'll have to earn your own living. That is if any publisher will accept your dreadful books!'

Charles looked at the floor. Tears began to trickle down his cheeks. Edward got up and left the room, slamming the door behind him. Joshua, who had been listening to the conversation, disappeared into another room.

Although Joshua loved his father, he was broken-hearted by the manner in which he had caused his brother to

30

despise him. He waited for Edward to go upstairs and approached his brother.

'I can't bear this any more,' said Joshua, adding, 'Please don't let Daddy's words make you hate me. I've never harmed you. All I want is for you to love me as a brother.'

'That can never be. I hated you since you were born and I'll go on hating you until I die.'

'Then you are a vindictive fool. The only person you are harming is yourself,' said Joshua.

Joshua did everything he could to improve his relationship with his brother, but failed. If anything, Charles's coldness became worse and his words more cutting. The relationship between Edward and Joshua grew closer even than before. Joshua developed a fascination for Russian literature. This subject was discussed throughout every meal, including breakfast. As Charles knew nothing about the subject, he was excluded from these conversations, like a foreigner.

It was about this time that Edward's elder sister, Rita, had become divorced on the grounds of her husband's constant infidelity. She had moved to a countrified, seventeenth-century house overlooking Hampstead Heath near the house where she and Edward had been born and bred. She was a professional concert pianist and had kept her maiden name. Edward had been extremely close to her since his childhood. She was tall and beautiful with brilliant, long, red hair, high cheekbones and sparkling green eyes. The news of her move delighted Edward. He took his sons to visit her for Sunday lunch one day.

Rita found Charles's behaviour, caused by his un-happiness, surly and bitter. She warmed to Joshua whom she found much more approachable. Rita did not under-stand brooding, bitter young men. She thought they were that way inclined because they were rude rather than unhappy. The boys were still twenty-five and twenty years old. When they and their father had Sunday lunch in Rita's house, Charles was just as much excluded from the conversation as he was at home. The unhappier he became, the more he was ignored. Joshua remained good-natured and forgave every rebuke he received from his brother, and spoke to him when Rita and Edward were talking. Charles's replies were monosyllabic and delivered without even looking his brother in the eye. Even his gait, before the family had sat down to lunch, was awkward and shuffling, like a drunk's.

The dining room at Rita's house had originally been seventeenth century, like the rest of the house, with dark, oak-panelled walls. She had found these oppressively gloomy and had had them painted white.

Rita, her brother and nephews were sitting in the drawing room, leading to the dining room. She was wearing a clinging, yellow silk dress which accentuated her lustrous, long, red hair and fresh, natural beauty.

The butler entered the drawing room and called the family into the dining room. Rita was the first to sit down. She did so with a flourish which set Joshua's blood on fire.

'Why have these bloody walls been painted white?' asked Edward confrontationally.

'Because I hate dark rooms. They depress me,' replied Rita. 'I'm the one who's got to live here, not you, I don't particularly like your house but I've never told you so up to now.'

'It's a shame,' said her brother. 'You've spoilt the room. It's no longer a period piece.'

There was a short silence. Charles found Rita's petulance towards his short-tempered father refreshing. He listened to the brief exchange, with his eyes lowered to the table. His aunt looked fleetingly at him, despising his inability to make conversation.

'Did you see *The News of the World* this morning, Aunt Rita?' asked Joshua.

'There's no need to call me "Aunt Rita",' said his aunt. 'Just call me "Rita".' She had taken a liking to the younger man and admired his brazen choice of reading matter. She continued, 'I read all the Sunday papers, including *The News of the World*. Was there something in today's edition which interested you?'

'Yes. The article about the footballer, Joe Morris, the man who was found plastered in a gutter in Charing Cross Road, after his doctors had told him that his next drink would kill him.'

'It didn't though, did it?' said Rita. 'I think it was disgraceful of the liver specialist, Professor Upton at King's College Hospital in Denmark Hill, to have agreed to be interviewed by *The News of the World* and to have volunteered so much information about his patient. The most dreadful thing of all was the way in which he even told the newspaper the results of his patient's liver function tests.'

As Rita spoke, Joshua became infatuated by her soft, deep voice and expressive manual gestures. She accentuated her good looks by wearing rings, one of which had a yellow stone, matching her dress.

'Is *The News of the World* your favourite Sunday paper?' she asked Joshua, smiling.

'Well, I know it shouldn't be, because it's not very high-brow, but I'm afraid it's the paper I enjoy reading the most.'

'What an honest boy you are! Your father said you had already written two books which the publisher, Lord Brook-Owen, had accepted. They're on sale in most of the bookshops, aren't they?'

'Only in some of them, Rita.'

'I've read both of them. I like your style. Your books are naughty but nice. I enjoy black humour.'

Edward rubbed his hands and looked proudly at his youngest son. 'They're naughty all right and his prose is stark and simple as well as funny. That's what makes his books sell so well. I wouldn't be surprised if he became a best-seller one day. I've told him that as well.'

Joshua turned to face Charles.

'That's a bit of an exaggeration. I've always enjoyed reading Charles's books. I know he emulates Ian Fleming. I think it takes a lot of courage to write about espionage. I wouldn't be capable of doing that,' he said kindly.

'How many books have *you* written, Charles?' asked Rita.

'What?'

'I said, how many books have you written? Also, don't say "what?" Say, "I beg your pardon?" It's more polite.'

'Four,' said Charles, still looking down at the table and grating his teeth. 'Twice as many as Joshua. He doesn't realize how hard I work. He doesn't respect my work, either.'

'Of course I respect your work, Charles,' said Joshua.

'Have any of your books been published, Charles?' asked Rita coldly.

'No. I've been unfortunate. Joshua's books have been published because he's been lucky. Skill hasn't played any part in his success. All he writes about is morbid, bloodthirsty stuff and pornography.'

'That's not a very attractive thing for one brother to say about another,' said Rita, 'particularly when Joshua said something nice to you just then.'

'If you find my conversation offensive, perhaps you would like me to go and sit in another room,' said Charles.

'I apologize for my son's rudeness,' said Edward. 'He's always been jealous of his younger brother because he can't face the fact that Joshua writes well when he can barely put a sentence together without hacking the English language to pieces.'

34

'I don't think that's true,' said Joshua, adding, 'I enjoyed reading the manuscripts of all four of Charles's books. They're more sophisticated than mine. He knows all about gadgets, engines and that sort of thing. I don't know anything about things like that.'

'There's no need to belittle yourself, Joshua,' said Rita. 'Is it worth sticking up for your brother when he doesn't thank you for it?'

'How do you expect me to thank him, Aunt Rita?' said Charles. 'My father has spoiled Joshua all his life and blamed me for things which weren't even my fault. At least I don't write books about death, perverted sex and violence.'

'Why do you think Joshua's books are published and yours are not?' asked Edward.

'I've already told you. Joshua's been lucky and I have not. His books were the first to be picked up off a literary agent's desk and sent to the right publisher at the right time.'

'Charles may be right,' said Joshua. 'Perhaps my good fortune is coincidental. Just because a writer gets a book published, it doesn't necessarily mean to say that that writer has more skill than an unlucky writer.'

Charles stared furiously at his brother. 'You won't get anywhere by sucking up to me,' he muttered.

Rita was moved by Joshua's loyalty towards his brother who failed to appreciate it. She realized that she loved Joshua and he, in turn, was captivated by her beauty. He had come to adore her.

Charles stared furiously at his younger brother. The more Joshua tried to be kind to him, the more he hated his patronage.

'The trouble with Joshua is that he's never been seen to do wrong. He's always comfortable with a pen in his hand rather than using a word processor. When a writer's self-confident, his prose, irrespective of his subject, becomes so animated that a literary editor goes for it, like a bolt of electricity. Even a morbid, pornographic book, written with skill the virtual size of a pin-head, can start an avalanche.'

'Have you got anything nice to say about Joshua?' asked Rita angrily.

'Not a lot. He's always sucking up to me. Because he's my father's favourite, I can't be expected to have any affection for him.'

'I don't suck up to you. I say these things because I respect you and I admire the way you write,' ventured Joshua sympathetically.

Rita turned to Charles. 'I can't bear your snideness towards Joshua, particularly as he's so loyal to you.'

'You're just biased, Aunt Rita.'

'How dare you speak to your aunt like that, Charles!' shouted Edward.

Charles got up, having dropped his knife and fork from a height, making a loud, clattering noise.

'I've had enough, Aunt Rita. I'm taking the bus home,' he said.

The atmosphere was more relaxed after Charles had left the house. Rita's conversation became ribald after her third glass of wine. The tone of her speech had an infectious effect on her brother and nephew.

Other articles in the tabloid press were discussed. Even the butler, who passed the pudding round the table, was shocked by the conversation and fled to the pantry in disgust.

'You couldn't have missed it, Eddy,' exclaimed Rita. 'It was all over page three of *The News of the World*. The article was about this lesbian who spent the night with a Cabinet Minister's cook.'

'I know that one,' said Joshua. 'What was it the woman said? I can't remember?'

36

'I'll tell you what she said,' said Rita, her speech slightly slurred. 'These were her exact words, "Waking up in the morning, and finding yourself lying beside a one-night stand, is about as squalid as entering a lavatory with an unpulled chain."'

Joshua laughed and ogled his glamorous aunt. His attraction towards her was magnetic.

'I wouldn't want you to think that the raunchy press is all I read on Sundays. I like the quality papers, as well. I leave *The News of the World* until last,' he said.

'Quite so,' said Rita. 'It's clear you've had a "sandwiches before cake" upbringing.'

Edward and Joshua stayed in Rita's house for the whole afternoon. Rita had a computer and typed into a programme about English monarchs which fascinated Joshua. Rita called up Edward II. The screen was covered with details of his reign, including the unpleasant manner in which he was murdered.

Rita typed the words, 'Tell us about his sex life'.

The screen showed the computer's way of answering the question: 'There is no such monarch as Hissex Life'.

Joshua loved Rita's spontaneous laugh. It was similar to the sound of a horse neighing, starting at the top of the scale and descending.

Edward went upstairs to rest in one of the spare bedrooms. Rita and Joshua were alone in the drawing room.

Rita's repertoire of anecdotes was endless. One of her stories was about a woman in a block of flats who rang the porter up at three o'clock in the morning, and rang him up again at four o'clock to apologize for waking him up at three o'clock.

Joshua turned to his aunt.

'I am hopelessly in love with you,' he said with extraordinary boldness, adding, 'but it breaks my heart to think it would be incestuous to marry you.'

'You don't have to marry me,' said Rita. 'I'd like you to be aware of one thing: You are to call this house your home at any time of the day or night. I know what the atmosphere must be like in your father's house. If you want to come here, you don't even have to ask me if you can come. Just ring me up to say you are coming. I get quite lonely, now that I'm divorced. Also, I haven't got any children. Your father knows how much your brother's behaviour depresses you. He wouldn't mind if you came to live here, as long as you visit him regularly.'

'I don't know what I would do without you,' said Joshua banally.

'An intelligent boy like you shouldn't make an idiotic remark like that. I can't stand sentimentality,' said Rita. The unexpected, sharp rebuke excited Joshua. In a masochistic way, the ticking off sent an electric, tingling sensation through his body and he felt himself go hard.

'Before you became a concert pianist, what else did you do?' he asked, after a pause.

'A lot of things, some of which I'd like to account for, others, not. I took a job as a nanny once. I lasted for ten minutes. I worked as a waitress and lasted for half an hour.'

'Why?' asked Joshua.

'I lost my temper with a man who was making sexual advances towards me. I emptied a pot of tea over his head. After that, I got a job in a hospital.'

'What sort of work did you do in the hospital?' asked Joshua.

'I was a medical secretary. That kind of work is exhausting but at the same time fascinating.'

'What does it entail?' asked the young man.

'Typing letters dictated by specialists to GPs, mainly. That alone takes up at least seven hours a day. Unless you work late, you can't finish your work on time. When you're working, other people come into your office from different departments and ask you to get up and look for patients' casenotes.'

'Couldn't you refuse?' asked Joshua.

'You get bunged out if you refuse. That's only part of your duties. You have to find patients' blood tests, put them into alphabetical order and clip them onto their casenotes. It's also expected of you to go to the medical records department and take casenotes out if a consultant asks for them. These aren't even in alphabetical order. They are found by numbers. Each number has six digits and you start by looking at the last two digits. You get giddy by the end of it. There are so many sets of notes that sometimes you have to climb up a ladder to get the right ones out. I need hardly mention the phone calls you have to deal with as well'

Rita continued, 'I was also in charge of the book in which I had to account for all the case notes that came into the office and went out of it. Many of the names in the book had the letters I.C. written alongside them. I thought I.C. stood for Intensive Care, meaning that the patients had been transferred to Intensive Care. No-one told me that the letters I.C. stood for "in cupboard", meaning the bloody case notes were in the cupboard in the corridor outside my office.'

'Why did you choose that kind of work?' asked Joshua, adding, 'It sounds absolutely dreadful.'

'Because I felt guilty about being wealthy. I went through a phase of wanting to live like a member of the working classes.'

'Why?'

'To justify my wealth guiltlessly, obviously. What a stupid question!'

'Couldn't you have gone straight into the music business? I should imagine that's pretty hard work as well,' commented Joshua.

'I could have done but I didn't feel quite right about it at the time.'

'How long were you doing hospital work for?'

'About eighteen months.'

'Did you leave because it was time for you to study music or because someone asked you to go?'

'The latter, my boy, the latter.' There was a twinkle in Rita's eye which excited Joshua. He breathed heavily.

He sat on the floor and leant against Rita's legs. She stroked his hair.

'Why were you told to leave?' he asked.

'The main reason was that my duties were in excess of what I was capable of doing, however hard I worked. Sometimes I stayed until ten o'clock at night. On one occasion, I overlooked a patient's dodgy result. I couldn't have been expected to get this right. Nor indeed should other medical secretaries have been called upon to do so. The result, on a small piece of paper, stated that a patient was quite ill. It was late at night. I was nearly falling asleep on the job and I failed to see the result.

'The consultant did not see the result either and the patient's illness became serious. The experience was absolutely horrendous. No one could have been expected to work like that and have only about four hours' sleep at night. Incidentally, the patient's illness became critical and he died. Another medical secretary, favoured by the consultant I was working under, blamed me for the patient's death. I felt badly enough without both a secretary and a consultant accusing me of causing someone's demise.

'Things came to a climax. The secretary and the consultant shouted at me, in unison: "That patient is dead because of you. I hope you're ashamed!"'

'How awful for you!' commented Joshua.

'Don't be stupid! It's obvious it was awful. I lost my

head – and my temper as well. I shouted, "What the bloody hell do you expect me to do about it? Bowl over to the mortuary and cross his sodding hands?" '

Rita's black-humoured wit enthralled Joshua. He felt so happy that he wanted to sing with joy.

Edward came downstairs after his rest and thanked his sister for the lunch.

'What about you, Joshua? Are you coming with me or do you want to spend more time with Rita?' he asked.

'May I stay with you, Rita?'

'Of course you can. Do you want to stay the night as well?'

'Only if that's convenient.'

Edward excused himself and put his hand on his son's shoulder. 'Will you ring me in the morning, old fellow?'

'Yes, I promise I will.'

'Don't keep Rita up all night, talking to her. She needs plenty of rest,' said Edward.

He got into his white Mercedes and turned on the ignition. He suddenly felt exceptionally sad because he knew he would be spending mealtimes alone with Charles, without Joshua being there.

Rita and Joshua had dinner at eight o'clock. They had a lot to drink and their conversation was as lively as it had been that afternoon.

'What I have to go through at home isn't easy,' said Joshua self-pityingly.

'That is what I am here for, to make you feel comfortable,' said Rita, adding, 'You seem to me to be an awful drip. You've got no guts, no manliness in you. That's why you're so scared of Charles.'

They had talked until after dinner and continued to do so until two o'clock in the morning. Joshua was about to go to bed.

41

'Would you like to stay here for a few days?' asked his aunt.

'For as long as you can have me. I'm getting more and more unhappy at home.'

Rita changed the subject abruptly. 'What wine do you think we should have for lunch tomorrow?' she asked, adding, 'we'll be having steak.'

'Oh, tomorrow's Monday. I never drink alcohol on Mondays.'

'Why not?' asked Rita.

'Monday is my liver's day off.'

'Oh? Do you dress it up in its best clothes and send it to the seaside with a bucket and spade?'

Telepathy between the aunt and nephew was such that Joshua often did not need to laugh to show that he was amused. The bond reminded him of that with his father, although his sexual attraction to his aunt was so virulent that it terrified him.

There was a waspish side to Rita. Sometimes, without warning, Joshua experienced the savage lash of her tongue. So extreme was her beauty and so perfectly-formed her lips that the sometimes cutting words ejected from them were dearer to the young man than the price of rubies. He felt as if hot oils were being rubbed into his skin and he occasionally wanted the abuse to be showered on him forever. It was because Rita knew the affect her quips had on him that her insults became frequent but were delivered with extreme affection, bordering on love.

Joshua and his aunt had lived together for a few weeks. He visited his father regularly, however. Rita was woken by her bedside phone at eight o'clock, one morning. It was a call from a public phone box. The caller was a cleaner who worked for Edward. Her name was Mrs Rushton. She was known to Rita. She was so hysterical that Rita had to hold the receiver a yard away from her ear.

'Can you repeat that? I can't hear you.'

'The whole house has been burned. Mr Edward died in the fire but there were no signs of Mr Charles being in the house. The safe has been ripped from the wall. I've got no idea how much was in it.'

Rita sat up with a jolt. Joshua was woken by the sound of the phone and did not need to be told that his father was dead and that Charles had been suspiciously absent from the house.

'How did it happen?' asked Rita.

'I've got no idea how the fire started. Everything's been burnt,' said Mrs Rushton between sobs, adding, 'I've already called the police.'

'Do you think Charles deliberately started the fire?'

'I've got no idea,' said Mrs Rushton. Rita hung up. She turned to Joshua.

'Get a bottle of brandy and two glasses,' she commanded.

'I'll do that. Where do you keep the brandy?'

'In the drinks cabinet. Where do you think, you cretin?'

'Yes, of course, I'll get them. When you get an awful shock, you get slow-witted, as well,' said Joshua.

'I can see that! Don't hang about. Once we've had some brandy, we'll both be able to think clearly. Mrs Rushton, the cleaner, said she'd called the police, before she rang me.'

The aunt and nephew drank half a bottle of brandy between them, even though it was quite early in the morning. Mrs Rushton had told the police where they could find Edward's next of kin. A police car, occupied by two detectives, pulled up in the gravelly drive leading to Rita's house. They were Detective Inspector Middleton and Detective Constable Brown. They went into Rita's drawing room. Detective Inspector Middleton did all the talking after he had introduced himself and his colleague.

43

'When did you last see Mr Flinton and his son?' Middleton asked Rita.

'Some time ago. I'm not sure exactly when. It was a Sunday. My brother and other nephew came to lunch. Charles, my elder nephew, got into a bait during lunch and got up and left,' said Rita.

'What was you talking about at lunch?'

'*The News of the World* mainly,' said Joshua.

'Oh, was you featured in it?'

'No.'

'Why was you talking about it? Neither of you look like the sort of people who read it.'

'It's a newspaper everyone reads,' said Rita. 'Some of us read it in public. Others read it behind closed doors.'

Middleton was confused. 'Has *The News of the World* got anything to do with the fire?' he asked.

'Mrs Rushton, the cleaner, said the safe had been ripped from the wall but she had no idea what was in it,' said Joshua.

'Would you mind answering my question?' asked Middleton abruptly. 'Has *The News of the World* got anything to do with the fire?' Joshua flushed to the roots of his hair.

'My brother and I are writers,' he replied. 'There is a lot of animosity between us. The arson has got nothing to do with *The News of the World.*'

'You're not Joshua Flinton, the writer, are you?' asked Middleton.

'Yes, I am,' replied Joshua modestly. 'I've only written two books so far.'

'My wife's very keen on your books. She's got both of them. She loves lurid, steamy stuff. If I bring them to you, will you sign them?'

'Yes, with pleasure,' replied Joshua demurely.

'There's one of the two books which my wife has a particular liking for.'

44

'Which one is that?'

'*Your Son Was Conceived in a Brothel.*'

'I'm sorry I chose such a bland title. I was under a lot of stress,' said Joshua self-consciously.

'How did your brother and late father get on?' asked Middleton.

'Very badly indeed,' replied Joshua.

'Have you got any reason to suppose that your brother deliberately started the fire?'

'It's hard to say as I wasn't there. He's bitter and vicious, so it wouldn't surprise me if he'd done it on purpose.'

'Was your father a heavy smoker?'

'Yes. About sixty cigarettes a day.'

Middleton removed a piece of paper from his pocket. He held it in front of Joshua. On it was a forward-slanting, scrawled note, which was barely legible.

'This was found on the top step, under a brick, leading to the house. Whose writing is it?' he asked.

Joshua took the note from Middleton's hand and held it up to the light. The handwriting was shaky, like a geriatric's. It read,

Salieri outlived Mozart in the end.

'That's my brother, Charles's handwriting,' said Joshua.

'Have you got any idea what that means? I've heard of Mozart, a piano basher, or something, wasn't he? I don't know the other name,' said Middleton.

'Salieri was court composer,' explained Joshua. 'He knew that his musicianship was inferior to Mozart's. That is to say, he knew that it was only mediocre. He was obsessively jealous of Mozart. He outlived him. He died in a lunatic asylum.'

'What has that got to do with the fire in your father's house?' asked Middleton, a trifle irritably.

'My brother is morbidly jealous of me because I got my two books published and he hasn't been able to get any of his books published,' said Joshua, adding, 'He's written four books.'

'What does your brother write about?' asked Middleton.

'Espionage, that sort of stuff. He imitates Ian Fleming.'

'Who the hell's Ian Fleming?'

'Jesus, Inspector, you haven't heard of Salieri. You haven't heard of Ian Fleming. Do you know who the Prime Minister is?' asked Rita rudely.

'Ian Fleming was a writer of spy thrillers. Many of them have been made into films,' explained Joshua. 'Ian Fleming's hero is called James Bond.'

'I don't know what the outcome of this will be,' said Middleton, changing the subject. 'We'll have to wait and see what the forensic lads have got to say.'

'Do you think my brother committed deliberate arson?' asked Joshua.

'It looks suspiciously like it, at the moment. It will depend on the results of our investigations though,' said Middleton.

Middleton and Brown left the house.

'Would you like me to play the piano, Joshua?' asked Rita. The impact of the news had not yet hit either of them.

'Yes, please,' said the young man.

'Choose something, anything you want.'

'Beethoven's *Appassionata*.'

'According to published stories about Lenin, the founder of the Soviet State, the *Appassionata* made him feel peaceful and gentle and devoid of class hatred, and the urge to get the NKFD, his secret police, to torture his victims and commit murders. Did you know that?' asked Rita.

'No.'

'You don't know much do you?' said Rita, adding, 'What a pity the old fool didn't listen to the *Appassionata* more often! I had communist sympathies in my late teens and I went to Russia. I saw a play about the Russian Revolution, called *Shyestoi Illooliya*. I've got no idea what that means. Felix Derzhinsky, the Head of the NKFD, bristled onto the stage wearing a tailored overcoat and he had a neat, pointed beard. The audience rose to their feet and gave the actor a standing ovation. They were clapping and cheering at a man playing the part of a sadistic serial killer.'

'My father was an authority on Russian literature. He was once an Oxford don,' said Joshua.

'I am aware of that. A sister is usually familiar with her brother's business,' said Rita coldly.

'Oh, sorry, I didn't know you knew.'

'It's hardly the sort of thing a sister would overlook, is it?'

There was a long pause while the aunt and nephew drank more brandy.

'I've got a fascination for Russian literature as well,' said Joshua. 'When I'm not writing, I spend a lot of time in the London Library, reading about the subject.'

'I didn't know you were that knowledgeable. Do you speak Russian?'

'Not yet. I've heard it's a very easy language to learn, contrary to what most people say. I want to have lessons so that I can read Russian poetry in the original. I think it's what my father would have wanted. The learning of the language will bring me closer to his memory.'

'Don't you want to have Charles found and punished first, seeing that he probably murdered your father?' asked Rita.

'Yes, I want him caught and sent to prison.' The young man's eyes were fiery and passionate. Rita had not seen the angry side of her nephew until then. It increased her maternal instinct.

'Charles will be found,' she said. 'Murder's difficult to

hide if the murderer's got no money. Edward told me that he had cut Charles out of his will. I doubt if Charles will even try to get as far as France. Does he speak French? I wish I knew what was in the safe which had been ripped out of the wall.'

'No, he doesn't speak French,' said Joshua. 'I doubt if he will try to get as far as France.'

'I would never have thought he'd been to a good school,' said Rita. 'I understand he went to the same school as you – the Westminster School for Boys.'

'Not even the best school in the world can make a scholar out of a wastrel,' said Joshua. 'He truanted most of the time and the only author he took an interest in was Ian Fleming.'

'Oh, that one,' said Rita obscurely. She went over to the piano. Joshua followed her.

'Come and sit with me,' she said.

Rita took the score of the *Appassionata* from a pile of music sheets and put it on the piano rack. She smiled at her nephew.

'You're going to be officer-in-charge of turning the pages.'

Joshua felt mortified. He feared his aunt would think he were a philistine.

'Don't worry. I know your father's death is beginning to hit you. Don't be embarrassed about crying if you want to. It's a sign of strength, even in a man.'

'It's not that, Rita. I feel such a fool.'

'Perhaps you are. Why do you think you are?'

'I've never had piano lessons. I can't read music, so I won't be able to turn the pages.'

'Oh? What's that got to do with folly?'

'Folly?'

'Yes. Foolishness or feeling a fool.'

'Perhaps because I said I read *The News of the World*,' said Joshua.

48

'What the hell has the miserable *News of the World* got to do with turning the pages?'

'It's not just that. I'm of no use to anyone, I'm afraid,' said the young man.

'You've already proved to me that you're pretty thick and cowardly but you do have a talent for the written word. Your fiction, though saucy, macabre and raunchy, is not too bad at all and gives pleasure to thousands of people. I like your books because you've got a galumph-like charm. Go and lie down on the sofa and I'll play the *Appassionata* for you. I've only got the energy to play the first movement, though.'

Rita played the piece while Joshua lay on the sofa. The onset of his grief started mildly and rose to a crescendo. He was hurt but at the same time attracted by his aunt's confusing, back-handed complements.

He wept unselfconsciously. His tears comforted him and made him feel that death alone would not divide his father's spirit from his own. He waited for Rita to finish playing the first movement of the *Appassionata*. She left the piano and sat down in another part of the room. Her silence made Joshua feel embarrassed about his inability to make intelligent conversation.

They ate the first part of their lunch in an awkward silence which was eventually broken by Joshua.

'I'm not as heart-broken as I thought I'd be if my father died. I feel he is still around me. I've got two things to live for: my continued contribution towards this country's heritage, and my ambition that I will find my evil brother and kill him.'

'I, too, believe that evil should be rendered for evil,' said Rita, adding, 'A Smith & Wesson, which a friend gave me when I was in America on a tour, could be useful to us, although there is no guarantee where timing is concerned. I'm a bloody good shot.'

'Where do you keep your gun?'

'In the top drawer of my bedside table.'

'Can I come up and see it?'

Rita laughed unnervingly. Her mocking manner took Joshua's mind off his father's death. They went upstairs to her bedroom. A light green, four-poster bed covered most of the room. The matching light green wallpaper was covered with Impressionist paintings. Rita opened the drawer and took out a ladies' gold-plated Smith & Wesson. She put her finger in the trigger guard and swivelled the gun round in the air, like a hussy from the Wild West. The gesture excited Joshua, as well as increasing his masochistic confusion.

'That thing's not loaded, is it?' he asked.

'Not now. It's easy to load, though. It holds six bullets in its chamber.'

Joshua was struck by the small size and delicate appearance of the gun. He tried to imagine a man using such a small weapon and having difficulty ramming his broad index finger into its trigger-guard. He thought of an average man and contrasted the size of his hands with Rita's tiny hands, enhancing her elegance and femininity. This was the first time he had studied her hands and not just the rings on her fingers.

Joshua and Rita lived together for roughly five years. Joshua had reached the age of about twenty-five. Their bitterness increased during that time, as did their grief. They thought seriously about finding Charles and killing him. Apart from the expression of their thoughts about their plan, they sat through most meals in silence. Joshua's sexual attraction towards his aunt, forbidden by the stigma of incest, intensified, and he was unable to understand whether it was pleasurable or painful.

'You told me once that when Charles sometimes goes

away from London, he rents a cottage in Cornwall, near a town called Liskeard,' said Rita. 'Can you remember saying that?'

'Yes. That's right. He does,' said Joshua.

'How does he get the money, if he's been cut out of your father's will and can't sell his books?'

'Charles has always been a miser,' said Joshua, adding, 'Although my father hated him, he gave us both an allowance since we were children. Charles once told me he'd been putting the money aside in a tin box which he kept under his bed. He must have saved quite a lot over the years. It was easy to do, as he had free board and lodging.'

The aunt and nephew had been sitting in the drawing room. Joshua was brushing Rita's long red hair.

'There's also the business about the safe,' said Joshua, adding, 'No doubt Charles is using whatever it contained to pay the rent for his cottage in Cornwall.'

'Just because someone's likely to have left London, it doesn't necessarily mean that that person is in Cornwall,' said Rita acidly.

'It *is* likely because I don't think there is any other place he'd be likely to go to. He only speaks English, so he wouldn't manage abroad.'

'Why do you think the police don't know about the cottage?' asked Rita suddenly.

Joshua finished brushing Rita's hair and arranged it in a tight plait. Part of her skin had been pulled away from her face, making her look ten years younger.

'You'll find this peculiar, Rita,' said Joshua. 'I deliberately refrained from letting the police know about the cottage in Cornwall. I didn't want them to get there before I did, because I like to see rough justice being done, not the rambling, plodding proceedings you get with the police and the courts. I'm the only person who's got some idea where Charles goes, if he wants to write or be alone. He rents a cottage in Cornwall as you know. The cottage is not far from Liskeard, as I said.'

Joshua continued, 'We should give him enough time to think the heat is off. If you want to catch a criminal, you leave him alone and relieve him of any suspicion that someone might be looking for him.'

Rita got up and paced up and down the room. 'That was one of your more intelligent remarks,' she said. She looked at her reflection in a wall covered with mirrors. Her psychological power over her nephew enthralled her. For his part, he enjoyed being humiliated by her, and thought he deserved to be psychologically injured in return for his cowardice and failure to stand up to his brother. He wanted his aunt to whip him but was too shy to express this wish to her.

'What are you thinking about, Joshua?' asked Rita.

'I can't live with the knowledge that I am a coward.'

'I wouldn't worry about that too much. It is true you are a coward. You can't change that. Once a coward, always a coward.'

'Is this really true?'

'Yes. Of course it is. You couldn't even stand up to your own brother.'

Rita was silent for a while and stared at her reflection in the mirror once more.

'Have you got any idea where this cottage near Liskeard is?' she asked.

'I'm not sure. The cottage is a small, slated, grey building with tiny windows. I saw a photograph of it once. Its name is *Goldeneye*. The word is ostentatiously painted in black letters about two feet high on the cottage's sloping roof. Charles chose the name, just because Ian Fleming's house in Jamaica was called that. If Charles had had any sense he would have painted over the letters by now.'

'How pathetic!' said Rita. 'You men are all the same.'

52

'When I saw the photograph of the cottage, there was a public phone box a few feet away from the front door. That's very unusual and conspicuous. He may have painted over the name of the cottage, but there'd be nothing he could do to get rid of the phone box,' said Joshua.

'You don't say!' said Rita in a cutting tone.

It took Joshua and Rita nearly three hours to reach Liskeard. They had been travelling in Rita's white Bedford van. She also owned a British racing green Porsche. She decided the Porsche would look too conspicuous.

They left the Bedford in the drive of the Lord Eliot Hotel at which they had arranged to stay. To their great astonishment and amusement, two men were fighting furiously in the bar. Their bone of contention was the ownership of a box of matches. Rita and Joshua then walked down the road to a pub which was nearly empty. They were dressed in shabby clothing, and until their accents were heard, they could have been taken for locals. A depressed-looking barman was drying beer glasses. Two men were sitting on bar stools, staring vacantly into space.

When the two Londoners approached the bar, the barman didn't look up. He continued to dry the beer glasses.

Rita spoke to him quietly in order to disguise her accent. She did all the talking.

'Yes, missus?'

'Two pints of lager, please.'

The barman gave Rita and Joshua the beer and took the money. They both drank fast in order to lessen their nervousness and ordered two more pints. Rita smiled and offered the barman a drink.

'Nice of you, maid. Much obliged. Are you tourists?'

'No,' said Rita. 'We've been staying with some friends locally. A man and his wife. We've got another friend living in the area. Does the name *Goldeneye* mean anything to you?'

'*Goldeneye?* I know that name. I say that because there's a phone box just outside a cottage with *Goldeneye* painted on its roof. It's a good twelve miles from here.'

'That's very convenient for the people living there, isn't it? That is if there's no phone in the house,' said, Joshua, stating the obvious. 'Do you know who lives there now?'

'I don't know if there's anyone there or not. There was a man who was a regular in here. He told us the name of his cottage was *Goldeneye*. He never spoke to anyone. He sat in the corner, writing. He used a laptop computer.'

'What did he look like?' asked Rita.

'Not entirely unlike your young friend, here, except that he had a thinner face and lighter hair.'

'Has this person left the area?'

'I don't know. He's just stopped coming here. All I know is the name *Goldeneye*. It attracted more attention that its occupant knew. It was painted in large, black letters on the slated roof of the cottage. I drove past it myself to visit my pals recently. There is a big dark patch where the letters were. If you want to go there, it's not hard to find. Take the road to Torpoint. Go on until you get to a village called Polbathic. After that, turn left and go up a steep, winding, narrow hill. 'Tis a right, fearsome, dismal place, with overhanging trees and no sunlight. 'Tis the scariest road in these parts. I don't want to, but I'm afraid I've got to warn you. Some say there's a jinx on that wood and on the cottage you're looking for.'

'It's all right. We're not superstitious,' said Rita with uncharacteristic politeness, adding, 'where do we go after we get past the steep hill?'

'When you get to the top of the hill, you follow the signpost to Anthony Village. Go on for a mile and you'll find a narrow lane off the main road. The cottage is on the left. It's the only cottage in the lane.'

'How do you know all this?' asked Rita politely.

'Our customer had had a bit too much to drink one night. He gave us directions and we took him home. It was then that we saw the phone box close to the cottage's front door.'

'Did he have a car?' asked Rita.

'No, I don't think so. He was a bit of a parasite. He was always hitching lifts, particularly when he was in his cups.'

The two Londoners thanked the barman. It was Joshua's turn to drive. Rita had written down the instructions and read them aloud. They came to the steep hill outside Polbathic. Rita thought it was a horrible place. She couldn't bear the absence of sunlight in the daytime.

Suddenly, the Bedford crashed inexplicably into one of the stone-based hedges.

'What the hell are you doing?' shouted Rita. Her nephew was lying with his face on the steering wheel. This startled her as he had hit his head on the steering wheel *before* the crash. Rita pulled the handbrake up and shook him violently.

'Joshua, are you OK?'

The young man was still unconscious and remained so for a few moments, before suffering the shock of regaining consciousness. He had had some kind of fit, resembling epilepsy.

'What's going on?' he shouted. He sounded lost, agitated and nauseated as fainters do when they come round.

'Don't you remember?' said Rita. 'You've been driving the Bedford. We were on our way to Charles's cottage. You got ill while you were driving. You fell unconscious and we ended up hitting the hedge.'

'I don't remember anything. Not since we talked to that barman. I've got no idea what he said.'

'You were taken ill while you were driving, as I said. Can you feel your arms, legs, hands and feet?'

'Yes, but I've got a terrible headache. When I woke up, I couldn't see very clearly at first.'

'We'll change places. I'll drive. I'm taking you to the A & E department at Plymouth General Hospital. I know roughly where it is because I've been there before, when my ex-husband was ill. I'm insisting that they give you a brain scan. Has this happened to you before?'

'No, but I found out that I'd had septicaemia when I was a baby and that I would have a personality disorder later on in life. I also found out that I might suffer from epilepsy as I got older.'

'Why the hell didn't you tell me all this before? You scared me stiff! I thought you were dying,' shouted Rita.

'I couldn't tell you. I was too embarrassed to tell someone like you that there could be something wrong with my brain.'

'Don't be daft, Joshua!' said Rita. 'Julius Caesar and Dostoevsky suffered from epilepsy, and they were both geniuses in their own field. Mind you, I knew there was something wrong with your brain all along. It was apparent the first time I met you.' She laughed. 'I was only joking, Joshua. Why were you embarrassed? I would have understood. If I had heart trouble, I wouldn't be too shy to tell you. How did you find out?'

'My father didn't want me to know. He thought it would upset me too much.'

'How did you find out? Wake up! That's the question I've just asked you.'

'Charles told me in the nastiest possible way. He was jealous of me because I was my father's favourite son.'

'Jesus, what a bastard!' said Rita. 'When you've been seen in the hospital, we'll do this journey again. I'm more determined than ever to find *Goldeneye*.'

The drab, grey streets and buildings in Plymouth depressed Rita and Joshua. Joshua leant forward, looking at the floor to avoid seeing what he thought was the ugliest city he had ever visited, apart from Birmingham.

Rita had forgotten the exact whereabouts of the hospital, and had to ask for directions several times, but to no avail. The people she met were even more drab than the houses they lived in. Eventually, a pedestrian gave her directions.

She parked the Bedford near Plymouth General Hospital. She was relieved to see Joshua walking normally, with animated eyes and a healthy complexion.

'I really don't understand why you brought me here, Rita,' he said, 'I feel OK. Perhaps I fell asleep because I was tired.'

'It was more than that. I had to shake you several times. If you'd only been asleep, you would have woken up straight away. That's not all that happened. While you were unconscious, your body was making jerking movements. It seemed as if you were having an epileptic fit.'

The humid A & E department at Plymouth General Hospital was dirty and overcrowded like an airless air-raid shelter. It consisted mainly of malingerers. There were a few road accident patients covered in blood, some screaming with pain. The more fortunate patients stared vacantly into space. A few of them looked hopeful. The majority looked like a collection of shabbily-dressed death-wishers.

Joshua and Rita sat down. They were both upset by the depressing atmosphere in the A & E department.

'I hate it here, Rita,' said Joshua. 'I want to go back and find the cottage.'

'That's out of the question, you stupid little boy!'

Three hours had passed before Joshua could be seen. A receptionist tapped the young man's details onto a keyboard. The keys had not been cleaned and chips of varnished nails had fallen between them. The receptionist wore no make-up and chewed gum noisily. She had rancid body odour which added to the stupefying unpleasantness invading the A & E department. Rita briefly explained to the receptionist what had happened in the Bedford, and also told her about the MRI scan performed on Joshua's brain when he was a baby.

The receptionist turned to Rita.

'What's your DOB?'

'What do you mean?'

'Date of birth?'

'How dare you ask me an insolent question like that? Next, you'll be asking me about my sex life.' Rita turned to her nephew. 'Wake up, Joshua. Tell this woman your date of birth.'

Joshua was embarrassed by his slow-wittedness and the way in which it had been shown in front of the woman he adored. He made an effort not to cry. He gave his date of birth. It was the twenty-second of June, nineteen fifty-nine.

A phone rang.

'Come on out of there and answer the bloody phone, Sue. Your tea-break's over!' the receptionist shouted. Another receptionist, looking even more unpresentable than her colleague, shuffled from behind a screen and took the call. She was followed by a nurse who turned to Rita. Rita gave the nurse all the relevant information about Joshua's case.

'So you say this young man had septicaemia when he was a baby,' said the nurse to Rita. 'And that an MRI scan of his brain done then showed that he would suffer from personality damage in adulthood. He also appears to have had an epileptic fit. Would you please go into cubicle five, Mr Flinton? Then take all your clothes off and put on this gown, I'll get an SHO to come and have a look at you.'

'It's been a bastard of a wait,' said Rita.

'That's because nerds with very little the matter with them overcrowd us all the time,' said the nurse.

'I insist on a consultant seeing him, not an SHO,' said Rita.

'A consultant? A consultant! What sort of hospital do you think this is? Don't you know anything about the troubles with the National Health Service since that bloody, mosquito-featured Tony Blair took over? Haven't you heard of New Labour?'

'How would you expect me to know anything about the National Health Service?' said Rita. 'I am a concert pianist. My name is Rita Flinton. Do you think I would expect you to know whether Handel's *Saraband Duo* would be better played in *C Minor* than in *D Minor*?'

Rita walked with Joshua to cubicle five. He felt belittled. He thought that his aunt was a far greater musician than he a writer. He undressed and put on the gown given to him. He climbed onto the stretcher-like bed, pulled the threadbare blanket up to his chin and lay on his back.

Rita sat on a scratched, plastic chair on Joshua's side of the curtain surrounding the bed and crossed her legs.

'Perhaps I should stop living with you, Rita,' said Joshua. 'I'm no more than a fatuous invalid.'

'Rubbish!' said Rita. 'You're a brilliant writer. Don't you dare say anything like that, again.'

'Why not, if it's true?'

'It's not true. If you say that one more time, I'll give you a good crack!'

A be-stethoscoped SHO came into cubicle five. He had a dishevelled look about him and his tie was loosened at the neck. His appearance attracted Rita as he had a shock of thick, unbrushed blond hair, aquamarine blue eyes and wore strongly-smelling aftershave.

'Hullo. I'm Dr Elliott. I'm SHO to Professor James. I

am aware of this patient's accident. Could you please tell me how you are related to each other?' He spoke with a heavy West country accent.

'We're lovers,' said Joshua aggressively. He had sensed Rita's attraction to Dr Elliot and resented it. He was also confused by her attraction to a scruffy-looking man with his tie loosened at the neck.

'I beg your pardon?' said Dr Elliott.

'Sorry, he was only joking. We are aunt and nephew,' said Rita. She looked amorously at Dr Elliott and angrily at Joshua.

'Do you want me to go outside the curtain?' she asked.

'Yes, if you would, please,' said Dr Elliott.

Dr Elliott pulled shut the curtain surrounding Joshua's cubicle, checked his eyes with a torch, looked into his ears and examined his tongue and throat. He listened to his heart, took his blood pressure and temperature, tapped his legs below the knee to check his reflexes and scratched the soles of his feet.

'What exactly happened?' he asked Joshua.

'I was driving up a hill. I suddenly fell unconscious. The van I was driving crashed into a hedge. I had a headache afterwards. I also felt agitated and frightened. I must have fainted. Miss Flinton thought I'd had an epileptic fit.'

'Is there a history of epilepsy in your family?' asked Dr Elliott.

'No, but I had septicaemia when I was a baby. I was in Great Ormond Street Hospital for Sick Children in London. Apparently, an MRI scan of my head showed that I would develop brain damage and a personality disorder later on in my life. The scan also showed I might suffer from epilepsy as well.'

'Have you had an epileptic fit before?'

'Nope,' said Joshua impertinently.

'Perhaps your attack was connected in some way to your illness as a baby, as well as something else, namely the personality disorder that you mentioned,' said Dr Elliott.

'Can you tell me anything more, doctor?'

'I can't tell you anything else yet. I know your last MRI scan was done many years ago. Ideally, I'd like to see that MRI scan as well.'

'They won't have saved it after all this time,' said Rita.

'No. It would surprise me a lot if they had.'

Dr Elliott left the cubicle to arrange an MRI scan of Joshua's brain and another test known as an electroencephalogram or EEG. Rita followed Dr Elliott who said the case was an emergency as Joshua had been the victim of a road traffic accident. He gave orders for Joshua to be put into a wheelchair and taken to the scanning department.

Rita waited until Joshua was due to have the MRI scan. Dr Elliott came towards her.

'Forgive me for asking. Are you Rita Flinton, the concert pianist?'

'I didn't know I was that well-known. So you recognized me?'

'I'm very keen on classical music and I attended one of your concerts in London about a year ago.'

'What was I playing? I've forgotten.'

'You played Rachmaninov's Second Piano Concerto in C Minor. The first movement is one of my favourite pieces.'

'Oh, Yes. That's right. It was at least a year ago when I played Rach II. It's a bastard of a piece to play. Even the composer found it difficult.'

'Shit, that's my consultant coming towards us, Professor James!' exclaimed Dr Elliott suddenly.

The Professor started talking to Dr Elliott.

'You really are looking awfully scruffy, Elliott. Can't you

do up your tie properly? Also, when did you last put a comb through your hair?'

'I only sleep one night in four, sir, I don't have time to smarten up. At night, I just turn in all standing.'

'What do you mean, you turn in all standing?'

'It's a naval expression. It means I get so tired I sleep in my clothes.'

Professor James was astonished by the manner in which Rita was lustily ogling Dr Elliott.

'I see,' he began. 'This young man, Mr Flinton, the one in the wheelchair – did you take his blood pressure, and if not, why not?'

'Yes, I checked it, sir.'

'What did the reading show?'

'It was a hundred and twenty over ninety-five millimetres mercury, sir.'

'Well done, Elliott. That's a little bit on the high side. The lady with the patient, is she his mother?'

Rita stretched out her hand, introduced herself and smiled at Professor James. He had a bone-crushing handshake.

'No, I am his aunt.'

Professor James suddenly looked very excited.

'I know you! You're Rita Flinton, the concert pianist, aren't you?'

'Yes.'

'I admire your work. I've got a few cassettes and long playing records recording your concerts. Could you excuse me for a moment. My colleague and I have got to talk shop. We won't be longer than about five minutes.'

'No, I don't mind.'

'Have you arranged for an MRI scan of the brain and an EEG to be performed on Mr Flinton yet?' Professor James asked Dr Elliott aggressively.

'Yes.'

'Good, Elliott. I see you've been pulling your weight

for a change.'

Joshua was later asked to get into a tube. It was like a mini spaceship. He had claustrophobia at first but recovered when the attendant played classical music.

Rita asked where the scanning department was, and when the MRI scan was over hers was the first face that Joshua saw.

'Are you pleased it's over?' she asked.

'Yes. It was a bit claustrophobic at first but I feel OK now.'

'Now you've got to have what is known as an EEG. It's quite painless. You lean back in a chair while jelly is put onto your head and rubber covered wires are fixed to your head as well. There will be a chart in front of you and a squiggly line going up and down on the chart. This will show the waves going through your brain,' explained Rita.

'How do you know all this?' Joshua asked.

'I've seen it done in most of the hospitals I worked in as a medical secretary.'

'Will it show what I'm thinking?'

'No. Even if it did, there wouldn't be much to show in your case, would there? All the machine does is study the waves passing through your brain. It's got nothing to do with your mind, only your brain.'

'But my mind *is* my brain.'

'For someone who's written books, your stupidity is incomprehensible. It will show if you're nervous and also whether you suffer from epilepsy. Another thing, don't grind your teeth. If you do, the test will confuse the person who looks at the result. The apparatus will make a crunching noise, and the test will be distorted. It will only have to be repeated, which would be an awful bore.'

Rita waited outside while Joshua was having the EEG.

The result came through after a long wait. One copy was kept by the A&E department. A second copy was given to Dr Elliott. The Flintons did not have a family doctor. Dr Elliott was the only connection they had ever had with the medical profession, apart from the doctor who had discussed Joshua's history when he was a baby.

While the EEG was taking place, a radiographer slapped Joshua's MRI scan onto an illuminated wall. He examined it for about five minutes. The typed report of the MRI scan, as well as the report of the EEG were given to Dr Elliott. The Flintons waited in the A&E department for another hour. Their spirits were lowered by a cup of tea which had been spilt on the floor. It was a disgusting sight.

Dr Elliott eventually ushered Joshua and Rita into his office.

'I might as well tell you of our findings,' he began. Rita leant forward and stared intensely at him, ogling his bright blue eyes and drinking in the strong smell of his aftershave.

Dr Elliott addressed Joshua. 'Both the MRI scan of your brain and the EEG show a significant case of epilepsy. I'm surprised you've only had one fit. There is also evidence that you will have quite a few psychotic episodes which will become more and more frequent as you get older. Have you had a psychotic episode before?'

'No. What can I take to control the epilepsy and the psychotic episodes?' asked Joshua urgently.

'There are a number of tablets you can take. I'm going to prescribe Tegretol Retard four hundred milligrams for the epilepsy. You should take three of these at night and two in the morning. This is a very high dose. I am also going to prescribe one tablet of Chlorpromazine a hundred milligrams at night to control your tendency towards psychotic episodes. Both the Tegretol Retard and the Chlorpromazine will make you feel drowsy and will help you to sleep. The two Tegretol Retard tablets, which you are advised to take in the morning as well, may make you feel a little drowsy during the day.'

'If I'm drowsy due to the pills, I won't be able to write my books,' said Joshua apprehensively.

'Don't worry. I'm going to give you something to counteract the drowsiness,' said Dr Elliott. 'It's a powerful stimulant, which also induces extreme euphoria and hurried behaviour. You may call these pills your "running sweets". The drug is called Dexamphetamine Sulphate, but it is more commonly known as Dexedrine. You should take no more than three of these every day. Dexedrine is known as "Speed" on the streets – that is to say, on the black market.'

'On the black market?' said Joshua. 'Do you mean it's illegal?'

'Not when a doctor prescribes it. It has a pleasant effect on the mood and makes you feel wide awake and extremely energetic. Some unethical people manage to get their doctors to prescribe it in bulk. It is an inexpensive drug and they sell it on the black market at a profit.'

'How shocking!' exclaimed Rita.

Dr Elliott wrote a prescription for the three lots of drugs.

'Where are you both from?' he asked eventually.

'London,' replied Rita.

'Find yourself a doctor who works in your catchment area. Give him this letter.'

Elliott got out pen and paper and wrote a brief note addressed 'To whom it may concern'. He put it into an envelope which he sealed and handed it to Joshua.

'There's just one more thing,' Dr Elliott asked Joshua. 'Yes?'

'Do you drive?'

'Yes. I love driving. It helps me to relax.'

'I'm afraid you'll have to stop driving altogether and you will have to give up alcohol,' said Dr Elliott.

Joshua thought about the manner in which Rita had often bullied and bludgeoned him for being an incompetent map-reader and regretted having to be a permanent passenger. The Flintons got into the Bedford. Rita was in the driving seat.

'We'll find a chemist for your prescription,' she said.

'How are we to know where to find one?'

'You're being stupid again. We'll ask for directions.'

Joshua leant out of the window and asked three pedestrians in turn. The third one said that there was a chemist round the corner. Joshua went into the chemist, handed in his prescription and when it was ready, he took three stimulants in one go with a glass of water. He got back into the Bedford. It had begun to get dark. He decided to wait until bed time before taking the other drugs which he had been prescribed.

'Ready to go?' asked Rita.

'Yes. I don't feel ill at all. I've just taken three of my "running sweets". I fell really energetic.'

'I remember there's a French restaurant near here,' said Rita, adding, 'I could do with something to eat. Are you hungry?'

'Not very, but I'd love to go to a French restaurant,' said Joshua.

'Good. Let's go and have dinner.'

Rita parked the Bedford near the French restaurant which had the unimaginative name, *Chez Nous*. Apart from an American tourist, gaudily dressed in an orange, red and yellow Hawaiian shirt and matching trousers, the place was empty. Twenty minutes had passed since Joshua had taken the stimulants which he referred to as his 'running sweets'. He had begun to feel euphoric.

66

An English waiter, who spoke with a heavy, bogus French accent, led Joshua and Rita to a table for two by the window. Rita asked for a gin and tonic when the menu was brought to the table. She ordered mussels and *Steak au Poivre* for herself and her nephew.

'May I have a gin and tonic, too?' asked Joshua.

'Bloody hell no! Didn't you hear what Dr Elliott said? You can't drink if you suffer from epilepsy. Do you want to have another fit? Have some tonic without the gin.'

A silence ensued. Rita lit a cigarette and blew a cloud of smoke into the air.

The American tourist came over and banged his fist on hers and Joshua's table.

'Say, lady, wouldja dunk yer cigarette out, please!'

'Knock it off! I'm in a smoking zone. If you don't like smokers, don't go to restaurants.'

'I don't care whether or not you're in a lousy smoking zone. I want you to dunk it out.'

Rita lost her temper with the American and shouted at him.

'I hope I'll only have to say this once! You're in someone else's country. I don't go to America and tell Americans what to do, so kindly don't come here and tell me what to do. Every time your fucking fellow countrymen come over here during tourist seasons, I have to go onto Prozac!'

Joshua had a giggling fit when Rita blew a cloud of smoke into the American's face. The American asked the waiter for the bill. He returned to where Rita was sitting.

'I've got news for you lady,' he began. 'My wife died of lung cancer not long ago, and I hope you get it too!' He paid his bill, got up and walked towards the door.

Joshua suddenly showed a display of artificial joy and exhibitionism, which was brought on by the stimulants he had recently taken. He followed the American to the door and tripped him up. He shouted, 'And we've got news for you, buster. Your wife was driven to excessive cigarette smoking because she was married to a repulsively dressed slob like you. You look as if you're covered in vomit.' Then, without warning, he broke into a loud, Vaudeville cockney accent.

'Sling yer 'ook, Guv'nor, or I'll 'ave yer duffed and yer bollocks bunged onto yer poxy missus's grave!'

The American whitened and staggered out. Rita had not listened to Joshua when he told her he'd taken his 'running sweets'. She burst into tears because she suspected that his psychotic episodes were already beginning. The aunt and nephew spent the night in a local three-star hotel. Joshua took three more stimulants the following morning.

When Joshua and Rita reached the steep, dark hill again the sun was shining and the place seemed brighter. An occasional ray of sun shone through the thick, imposing trees.

Rita found the signpost to Anthony village and drove on for about a mile. She turned into a narrow lane off the main road. She drove on and eventually found a slate roofed cottage in the lane. The cottage looked in a poor condition. A lot of the slates had fallen off the roof.

Just outside the cottage was a red phone box with some of its glass smashed.

Rita and Joshua got out of the Bedford.

'Can you see a large dark patch on the sloping roof of the cottage?' asked Rita.

'Yes. It's even blacker than the slates. It's as if the area had been covered with thick black paint on purpose.'

'OK, Joshua. Let's see what we can find. The cottage may be empty. If it is, we'll have to break in and look for information about Charles's whereabouts.'

Suddenly, a light was turned on in the cottage.

'What will happen if Charles is there and might try to kill us?' asked Joshua.

'That's another of your daft questions. I'm not carrying a loaded Smith & Wesson just for the hell of it.'

Joshua felt another strange twinge. It was like toothache and it hit him whenever his idol snubbed him, while being oddly pleasurable.

There was an upside-down brass horse-shoe on the only door of the cottage. Rita banged it against the door several times.

The door opened very slowly, as if the inhabitant of the cottage were terrified of visitors. The footsteps Rita and Joshua heard sounded like those of someone who was either lame or drunk. As the person came closer to the front door, a heavy wheezing sound could be heard.

A woman opened the door with a flourish. She looked strange and suspicious. She appeared to be about sixty years old. Her greying hair was scraped back from her face. She was overweight and was wearing a dark brown cotton dress with a white collar. She had tiny eyes which prevented Rita and Joshua from seeing what colour they were. In contrast to her austere clothing, she had an over-made-up face like an ageing prostitute's.

'Who are you?' asked the woman.

'Am I to understand that a certain Charles Flinton either lives here or has been living here?' asked Rita.

Another woman came to the door. She was dressed garishly, like a character out of an opera. Like her companion, she had an over-made-up face.

Pots and pans hung from the walls. Because of the tiny windows, the cottage was unwelcoming and forbidding. There was a sinister aura about the place, and there were no chairs to sit on.

'Who are these people and what do they want?' asked the second woman.

'They'm strangers, They'm not from round here. They'm seeking information, I think. I don't want 'em here but if we don't bring 'em in, they'll never go away.'

'My name's Rita Flinton and this is my nephew, Joshua,' said Rita, adding, 'Joshua is Charles Flinton's younger brother.'

The woman ushered the aunt and nephew into the cottage. There was no sign of welcome, only a hostile, beckoning gesture. 'I'm Elsie Earle and she's Jill,' said the opener of the door.

'May we sit down somewhere?' asked Rita.

'Can 'ee see any chairs?' asked Elsie in an exceptionally harsh tone.

'I won't take up more of your time than is necessary,' said Rita. 'Has a man called Charles Flinton been staying in this cottage at any time?'

'What do I tell 'em, Jill?' asked Elsie.

'Does it matter any more what we tell 'em? Tell 'em anything you like,' said Jill. 'I doubt if we'll be seeing 'im no more.'

As she spoke, Jill moved her foot. A high pile of Ian Fleming's novels tumbled onto the floor from against the wall. The books were soggy and hardly readable. A wad of damp papers fell onto the floor from behind the books. Rita picked one of them up.

'You've got no business touching them papers,' said Elsie.

'Sorry, we've got to. We're part of Charles's family and Joshua, here, is his brother, as I said.'

Elsie looked at Jill. The two women seemed too frightened to resist their visitors. Elsie got out a clay pipe and lit it. The two women sat on the floor.

Rita started to turn over one of the loose papers which had fallen from the pile of Ian Fleming's novels. Charles had been writing a book. The handwriting was identical to the handwriting on the piece of paper which Detective

70

Inspector Middleton had picked up after Edward's house had been burned down. She turned to the first page and read the extract out loud.

Poor old Klaus was wretched and not like James Bond. Bond was confident and together. He was stronger because his father had probably been nicer to him than Klaus's father.

Klaus served in MI5. He excelled, but he had a permanent death wish.

Klaus was good at everything, even if his memory of his tyrannical father haunted him. Everyone looked up to Klaus, unaware of his chronic misery.

Klaus was the best at finding the birds. He got through at least six a week. Klaus was a fantastic stud but he hated sex and had never had an orgasm in his life.

Klaus had the brain of Einstein and the looks of a Greek god. He was a sportsman and an expert in every sporting field but hated the activities he participated in.

I am like Klaus. I was bullied and persecuted by my father all my life. That is why I don't want to live. The problem is I haven't got the guts to commit suicide.

'Can I see that piece of paper, Rita?' asked Joshua. Rita passed the piece of paper to Joshua.

'If that's how your brother writes, it's no wonder he can't find a publisher,' commented Rita.

Joshua read the writing on the piece of paper which Rita had passed to him and had a giggling fit.

'What's so funny?' asked Rita.

'It's Charles's ghastly style of writing. First, he writes about what seems to be his main protagonist, using very monotonous and repetitive language. He starts off by using the third person and then tells the reader about his problems using the first person,' said Joshua. 'He's so pathetic and incompetent with his pen that this document is absolutely hilarious. Reading it has really cheered me up. It's made my day.'

'When was Charles last seen? Do you know where he went?' Rita asked Elsie.

Elsie held out her hand, palm-upwards. Rita put a fifty-pound note into it.

'I first met Charles a long time ago. He had rented this place on and off for a while, even before I met him,' said Elsie.

'How did you meet him?' asked Rita.

'We was up Plymouth way. Me and Jill had an old van,' said Elsie. 'We was looking for fellas from the ships. This place was the only place where we could furnish the sailors with "Specials". That's because we was in the middle of nowhere and the Law couldn't find us. It was upstairs where we did most of our trade. Sometimes, we worked in the back of the van.'

'What's this got to do with Charles Flinton?' asked Rita impatiently.

'He was walking down the street near the docks one night. He was attracted by our heavily made-up faces. He took us to a café and bought us tea. He told us his trade was writing, but that work was slack and he asked us if we needed someone to protect us. We were prostitutes and he was our pimp. We moved in with him and we gave him a cut of our earnings in return for his protection. He agreed to drive the van which we nicknamed the "Sado-mobile" because sometimes we worked for sailors in the back of the van; that was when we wasn't working here in Charles's cottage. A few sailors got in the van almost every night. We told 'em we only did Specials, which cost a lot more than ordinary sex and some of them said that that was precisely what they wanted. We'd never felt safe before we met Charles. Sailors can get quite rough and if they want Specials, they can get exceptionally heavy with women. Because Charles's writing trade was slack, he agreed to continue being our pimp. It was OK at first but then we had trouble.'

'Trouble of what nature?' asked Rita abruptly.

'He insisted on getting a higher cut of our earnings. He warned us that he'd shop us, by going to the Law if we didn't do what he asked.'

'This is blackmail. It's quite disgraceful,' said Rita. 'Did you agree?'

'We had no choice. Then one day we got talking to a newsagent in Plymouth, a pal of ours. The front page of one of the newspapers had a close-up picture of Charles, giving his full name. It said he had been "missing" for some time and that he was wanted by the police for questioning about his father's death, caused by arson, up London way.

'We bought the paper and we told Charles we'd turn him in if he carried on insisting on taking extra money off us. A docker, having a good time upstairs with Jill, heard me and Charles arguing downstairs. The docker went downstairs and snatched the paper from my hand. He shouted, "I've heard about this case. It's 'im!" Charles lost his head and hit the docker on the head with a poker and killed him.'

'Jesus!' was all Rita could think of saying.

'What happened to the docker's body?' asked Joshua, who had been quiet until then.

'You don't need to know that,' said Elsie. 'It was disposed of, all right. No one can find it. Anyway, it's decomposed by now, ain't it?'

'Did Charles dispose of it?'

'Yes.'

'When he left here, did he say where he was going?' asked Rita.

'He said he might be going back London way eventually, once the heat was off. He had changed his appearance by shaving his head, and he changed his name to Nick Robinson. There have been posters of Charles Flinton all over Plymouth.'

'How long ago did he say he intended to go back to London?' asked Rita.

'Nigh on a couple of years ago, I'd say,' replied Elsie, adding, 'Word went round that he'd picked up a barmaid in a pub in Polbathic and that he'd been having a long fling with her.'

'And you've heard nothing since?' asked Rita.

'No. Much earlier he had painted the name of this cottage in thick white letters on the slates. He called the cottage *Goldeneye* for some reason. When things got hot, he painted the letters over with thick black paint.'

'I thought he'd lived in the cottage longer than you,' said Rita.

'He 'ad, on and off. Then he went away. I don't know where he went. Maybe he's still with the barmaid in Polbathic.'

'There's another question I'd like to ask you,' said Rita.

'Aye?'

'Someone said there was a jinx on the steep, wooded hill near this cottage.'

'There's one on the hill, all right,' said Elsie. 'If I were you, I'd take another route if you want to go back home without coming to harm.'

'Is there any chance of my going upstairs?' asked Rita.

'No!' shouted Elsie hysterically.

'Oh, no, not no. Yes!' exclaimed Rita. She rushed upstairs, supporting herself with the unsafe bannisters, using both hands.

'You're to come down and come down now!' shouted Elsie, who looked agitated and flustered. She tried to run after Rita but was not fit enough.

Joshua heard a terrifying shriek from one of the upstairs rooms. It was Rita.

Charles had painted some caricatures of his father. They showed a man in an advanced state of decomposition. Rats, meticulously outlined, were shown gnawing at his body.

Rita came downstairs, shaken.

'Come on, Joshua, out of this place, now!' she shouted.

Rita was angry when superstitions were imposed on her and resented Elsie's warning of danger. She regarded herself as an intelligent woman, whose intelligence was insulted by having to listen to what she called 'bloody old wives' tales'.

'Come on, Joshua, get in the Bedford. We're going back to Polbathic to investigate the pub there.'

'I want to drive,' said Joshua.

'You can't, you stupid little boy! Not after what you were told at the hospital.'

Rita drove the Bedford slowly down the steep, dark hill. Joshua felt a sudden black mood descending on him as if something were trying to advise him of imminent doom. The mood was caused because the effects of the 'running sweets' which he had taken a few hours earlier, had worn off.

A motorbike, whose rider was driving at about seventy-five miles an hour, came towards the Bedford. Rita turned the steering wheel towards the rock-hard hedge. The steering wheel crushed her ribs. One of her ribs perforated her heart which killed her outright. The motorbike rider did not stop to report the accident. Only a passing cyclist reported it on his mobile phone.

Joshua was in such a state of shock that Rita's death numbed him. All he knew was that the accident had occurred near the place where he had had the epileptic fit.

He did not remember being taken back to Plymouth

General Hospital. His amnesia was on the side of his sanity. He had been picked up by an ambulance which took him back to the hospital. He was there for a few days and was looked after on the psychiatric ward.

He discharged himself after a week, took the train to London and went back to Rita's house and took a large dose of the 'running sweets' which he had been prescribed. He decided to give up taking the Chlorpromazine for his reported psychotic disorder, as well as the Tegretol Retard for his epilepsy, as both these medications caused him extreme drowsiness whenever he needed to write. He lay on his back on the sofa and after about twenty minutes he noticed a dramatic elevation in his mood despite Rita's death. He felt more secure because he sensed that she was all around him. He went into the drawing room which was awash with daylight. He sat down and started to use his old typewriter, like the one his father had used, as like his father he did not like word processors. He took a thick wad of paper from the drawer of the desk he sat at. He fed a piece of paper into the typewriter and did what he had longed to do for some time.

The keys of his typewriter clacked effortlessly. The book he had started, loosely based on his deification of his caustic aunt, seemed to be writing itself without guidance from his fingers. He delighted in his sudden literary skill and the 'running sweets' initially thrilled him. In his masochistic state he was proud of receiving every verbal missile that Rita had showered on him, because of her love of teasingly humiliating him. So ashamed was he of his cowardice during his childhood and of his failure to stand up to his brother that he yearned for punishment and insults from a beautiful and brilliant woman. He worked, almost without rest, for ten days.

As far as Joshua was concerned, Rita was no longer dead, although her funeral had taken place three days before.

She was immortal and inviolate. She would never die and the memory of her sometimes cruel tongue exorcised Joshua's shame of his failure to stand up to his brother.

His father had told him once that it was more painful to hate the dead than it was to love them. However, his love for his aunt was becoming even greater than it had been while she lived. His self-hatred made him wallow in the memory of her acid quips, as if they had been wine.

On the other hand, he shied from the memory of her frequent care and warmth towards him. To him, her cruellest words were her kindest ones.

He felt her presence, not in the graveyard where she lay buried, but in the house. He could hear her brisk movements and her soft, deep voice and feel her flouncing in front of the mirrors.

He took more of Dr Elliott's 'running sweets' and realized he would soon need a repeat prescription from his new doctor in London, Dr Bennett. Dr Bennett was five foot eight inches tall and had wavy, dark brown hair parted in the centre. He was sympathetic when Joshua visited him and on reading Dr Elliott's letter he recognized his patient's need for the 'running sweets' alone because the Tegretol Retard for his epilepsy and the Chlorpromazine for his potentially psychotic states were interfering with his writing. If rightly or wrongly, Dr Bennett had strongly recommended that he use the 'running sweets' alone. He had emphasised to Joshua that he take no more than three of these a day, however. Despite Dr Bennett's advice, Joshua feared that he might have another epileptic fit, so he took the Tegretol Retard but at a much lower dose than Dr Elliott had originally prescribed for him. The adjustment in his medicines appeared to suit him. He threw the Chlorpromazine away.

He typed for long hours every day. While he was taking a break, the title of the book came to him lucidly. He had thought for a long time about his heroine's name. He chose 'Lucinda Maloney'. She would be the omnipresent Rita. He wanted to make Rita immortal by committing her to the printed page, so that he could open the book and find her any time he wanted her. His decision comforted and delighted him and increased his strange feeling of security.

Despite his solitude, he lived in Paradise for the following two weeks. He increased his intake of the 'running sweets' every day, despite Dr Bennett's and Dr Elliott's advice that he should only take three a day. They soon began to induce violent mood swings, a distorted vision of reality and confusion about his heroine whose existence in the book had soothed and comforted him earlier.

Try as he did to deify Rita, he began to lose his grip on her physical beauty and awkwardly complex and incomprehensible personality. His main female protagonist, whom he had called Lucinda Maloney, started to mutate into another equally beautiful woman who was distanced from Rita, because unlike Rita, Lucinda was synthetic, like a life-sized, pumped-up doll from a sex shop. At least Rita had lived, even if she had died. Lucinda had never been conceived, never been born and had never assumed human form. The 'running sweets' had caused Joshua to lose control. He forced himself to love his new protagonist, and face the fact that she was not real. He tried in vain to convince himself that Lucinda was a clone of Rita, but the truth kept plaguing him.

After about a month, he realized that something else was wrong. His use of the 'running sweets' had become out of control. He increased his intake further, much higher than the dose that the two doctors had recommended. Instead of giving him relief, the 'running sweets' began to cause him deadly attacks of melancholia after a few hours when their effect wore off. One attack was so severe that he had to lie down on Rita's four-poster bed in total darkness for three days. All he swallowed was water.

He got up, thinking that his mental state would get back to normal if he took another palmful of 'running sweets'.

He took an even higher dose than before. He took more sheets of paper out of Rita's desk drawer. He assumed that the permanently rejuvenated and immortal Lucinda would comfort and stimulate him, and that he would be able to re-read what he had written and feel ecstatic once more. He was beginning to accept the fact that the deification of Rita was impossible, and he concentrated his work on Lucinda, whom he would make into a different kind of goddess. He started reading at the beginning, mouthing what he had considered to be his sacred words about sacred flesh inviolate.

He put the manuscript down and stared into space for a while. He wondered why he had stopped reading. Suddenly, he felt as if he had been struck by an invisible iron bar. He lay down on Rita's four-poster bed once more. He was having a horrible and terrifying hallucination, brought on by the wearing out of the excessive dose of the 'running sweets'. He imagined he felt a slimy, black creature crawling over him, starting to cover his feet before working its way upwards to his neck. The creature felt cold, heavy and slippery.

He rolled onto his side in order to shake it off but it was stronger than he was and clung to him like a giant leech.

What terrified him was his wrongful conviction that it was real. It was made worse by the fact that it had neither a head nor limbs. It was a living blanket of foul-smelling black slime.

It slithered away from his body as quickly as it had

come, however. It wasn't until it had gone that he was struck by the worst fit of gloom he had ever had in his life. He thought that even the rancid slime was preferable to the gloom. He had a shivering fit which lasted for about twenty minutes.

He got off Rita's bed and looked at his manuscript once more before lying down again. A nightmarish thought, which he could not drive away, invaded him.

He feared that the manuscript was in some way responsible for the hallucination that he had had. It didn't occur to him that his gloom descended on him because the 'running sweets' were addictive and were regularly wearing off. It was not until about an hour had passed that he knew that the blanket of rancid slime was his crippling melancholia in a physical form.

He thought about his book once more, and felt as if an imaginary iron bar were violently descending onto his body.

He was about to pick up the manuscript but did not need to. He knew something in it had turned against him, and that was the knowledge that Lucinda wasn't real. She could neither be touched nor caressed, and what was even worse, she could not be physically loved.

Joshua tried to switch his mind off but the invasive, odious thoughts which he could not drive away descended on him. He would have preferred it, had they been locusts burrowing into his brain.

He remained at Rita's house, troubled by his heroine for about eighteen months.

One evening, his thoughts were continuing to tell him something but he refused to listen. They tormented him for about two hours until he grew weak and gave in. He took another dose of the 'running sweets'.

It was then that he knew that the very nucleus of his life

had exploded like an atom. At first, he had considered Lucinda to be a character in a book to be loved and visited whenever he wished to look at his work. What he had not wished to fully accept was the fact that a mere character in a book, irrespective of its writer's skill, can never be re-created on an earthly plane. It can only be loved and appreciated as print on paper. The thing which added to Joshua's gloom was the wearing off of the 'running sweets' once more. He wanted more and more of them and took more and more of them. He was up to taking twenty a day.

Moreover, Lucinda had not been conceived of a man and a woman. Her only parent was Joshua's typewriter ribbon. He was frightened by his failure to realize this before and wondered if the personality disorder predicted on the two MRI scans of his brain was beginning.

It dawned on him that there was only one thing he could do to prevent himself from committing suicide. As Lucinda was not a real person, and as the attainment of this knowledge had taken the meaning from his life, he decided he would have to kill her.

He would not do this immediately as it would mean his destroying the book, and literary abortion was a smouldering anathema to him.

He thought that there could be a chance of his exorcising his demons, once he had killed his non-existent love.

The idea of killing her gave him hope. He told himself that he would work the longest hours he could, to ensure the rapid eruption of what he saw as the plague sore destroying him. Either he or Lucinda would have to die. He hoped he would not be the one to die first. He knocked back a vast number of 'running sweets' and got up and typed in the centre of a blank page, the words, 'THE KILLING OF LUCINDA MALONEY'. This he considered to be an excellent title.

As he took even more 'running sweets', his writing

shifts became longer. He would not let anything come between Lucinda and his need to destroy her, in order to save his limited sanity.

Suddenly, he felt weak and dizzy, which alarmed him. His 'running sweets' were not working properly, despite his greatly increased dose, and they were his ink, and his ink was the rope with which he would hang Lucinda. Without his ink, he could do nothing. To give himself strength, he leant over his typewriter keys and managed to write a disciplinary note in capital letters to himself in the centre of the page.

I SHALL NOT REST UNTIL MY WORK IS FINISHED.

He slumped over the typewriter and slept for a while. When he woke up, he saw the words staring him in the face.

Approximately three years passed. Joshua had not engaged any domestic staff and lived on take-away foods. The house, which had formerly belonged to his idol and which had been clean, neat and tidy, was filthy and untidy. He had sacked all Rita's staff. The lawn had not been mown. His habits from day to day were like clockwork, however. When he was too tired to type any more, he carried Rita's ghetto-blaster upstairs to her bed. He lay on his back, holding it to his chest. He liked to listen to Radio Four for about two hours before he went to sleep for a few hours every night.

Suddenly, a jolt passed through his body like a flash of lightning. He sprang from his lying position, let out a shout and turned the volume up. He could feel the beating of his heart and lifted the ghetto-blaster to his ear. He listened, thunderstruck.

'This is an SOS message. Would Mr Joshua Flinton, last

heard of in north London, some time ago, please contact the Royal Free Hospital in Hampstead, London, NW3, where his brother, Charles Flinton, is dangerously ill.'

Joshua hailed a taxi and asked the driver to take him to the Royal Free Hospital. He had never been there before. It struck him from the outside as looking similar to one of the terminals at Nice Airport, which his father had sometimes taken him and his brother to on their holidays.

He went through an automatically-opening door and turned right. The grey carpet leading to the reception desk was unhoovered and covered with cigarette butts and rolled-up pieces of paper.

He identified himself to the receptionist and gave his brother's name and date of birth. He was born on the twenty-fifth of April, nineteen fifty-four. The receptionist appeared slow-witted and bored. She tapped out Charles's name on a green screen with black letters on it. She directed Joshua to a high-rise floor, where a nurse showed him to an isolated room next to a ward. Joshua hardly recognized his emaciated brother who had wires and monitors attached to his body. The shock had taken Joshua's mind off his 'running sweets' temporarily.

'So you sent for me?' he said, without preamble.

'Yes. I refused to give the name of my next of kin until I knew my time was up. The SOS message I sent out on the radio wasn't the only one I sent out. I sent out about six messages in all. I want to ask you for your forgiveness for my dreadful behaviour towards you when we were children, and to thank you for your kind remarks when we had lunch with our aunt that day.' Charles paused, stared into space for a moment and added in a shamed tone, 'Not only that, for burning our house down and killing our father.'

Joshua sat on a chair by his brother's bed. He took his

hand and was appalled by the thinness of his skin and the needle marks on his hands and arms.

'Even though you burnt the house down and caused our dear father's death, there's something in me which can forgive your crime,' said Joshua. 'You've been punished already. I never kick people who are bleeding in the gutter, when I'm still lucky enough to have my health – my physical health at any rate,' Joshua added as an afterthought.

'I expect you want to know what brought me here,' said Charles.

'Yes, I do. Why are you here?'

'I've smashed my liver. I'm afraid it's terminal.'

'Oh, dear, I'm very sorry indeed to hear that,' was all Joshua could think of saying.

'I couldn't publish any of my books,' said Charles. 'I gave up hope. I did odd jobs here and there. I became a pimp for two kinky prostitutes in Plymouth. I had a fling with a woman I met in a pub in Polbathic. Then I moved back to London. The first place I went to was a public lavatory in Piccadilly Circus. I got addicted to heroin and I used shared needles. I knew that Green Park was a good place to socialize, if you can call it that. There are always junkies of both sexes there.

'I got over the fence, into the park. After doing this every night for a few weeks, I met a woman called Monica. We've got a lot in common. She's a painter of modern stuff, something I don't really understand. She comes from the same background as us. She is convinced that she will be famous one day and have exhibitions all over the world.

'Fame is a matter of luck, not necessarily talent. She always tells me that. She could have been beautiful, had she not succumbed to heroin. She made an effort to give it up for a while. The bond between us got very deep and became physical. One day she said she was pregnant

84

and that she was sure the baby would be harmed by the heroin if she went on using it, so she went into rehab for a short period of time.

'She was prepared for the birth. She lay down on her back in Green Park, one warm summer evening. She had very few contractions and a baby boy was born. We chose the name Arthur Richard for him. I knew I was dying and would never see my son grow up but Monica managed to keep the baby healthy. It wasn't until some time after the birth that she went back onto heroin, though. The baby wasn't affected.'

Joshua felt very depressed. 'I'm so glad to hear that,' he muttered after a pause.

'Before they allocated a bed for me here, I consulted an adoption agency,' continued Charles. 'I told them about you. I was hoping you were still alive. Then I started sending the SOS messages out. I thought there might be a chance of my finding you in the end.' Charles continued to talk mechanically. 'Monica and I went to an adoption agency together. I told the interviewer that I had a kind, responsible brother who was well-off. I didn't want to mention what was shown on your MRI scan done when you were a baby. The woman behind the desk actually recognized your name and said that although she found your books disturbing, morbid and bloodthirsty, she loved your handling of the written word.'

Joshua crossed and uncrossed his legs on the uncomfortable chair by his brother's bed.

'Thanks for that, anyway,' he murmured modestly.

'If you are willing, Monica would very much like to meet you. I'll write a short note of introduction. She said you'd have to sit before a panel, to make sure you'd be a suitable guardian for my son. If you really would like to look after Arthur, and go to the adoption agency concerned, I'm sure they would find you acceptable. Tell me, honestly, would you like to look after Arthur and bring him up and save him from living in an orphanage, or would it be too much for you?'

'Of course, I'd like to have him. I've always wanted a child. I live alone now and a child would cheer me up,' said Joshua. He was aware of the fact that his 'running sweets' had plateaued but that he could not give them up entirely.

'Good lad,' said Charles. 'Let me ring the woman I know. Her name's Charlotte Williamson. I'll ring her now. I'm too ill to move, but I'll see if she's able to come over here and meet you. Her phone number is 0207 794 1970. Will you dial it for me on the pay phone by my bed?'

Joshua had some coins on him and dialled the number. Charlotte agreed to visit the brothers later that day. She was struck by their mild facial resemblance and obvious genuine desire to give Arthur a stable home.

Charles signed some documents, stating his wish that his son be adopted by his brother. As he signed his name at the bottom of each sheet, he was too weak to sit up and lay on his back.

Joshua agreed to visit the adoption agency and was interviewed by a panel, consisting of a man and two pernickety women. All three had been informed by Charlotte that Joshua was respectable and well-off and was keen to interview a number of nannies before taking Arthur to his home. They knew nothing about his addiction to 'running sweets' or what was foretold on the MRI scans of his brain.

He was told that Arthur would be temporarily in Monica's care until a reputable nanny could be found, but there was no mention of the baby's whereabouts.

Joshua went back to the hospital the following day. Charles was sitting up, supported by pillows.

'Doesn't Monica resent my adopting Arthur?' asked Joshua.

'I've talked to her about it. She never really wanted a baby and hates the idea of being a responsible mother.'

'Where's Arthur now?' asked Joshua.

'He's with his mother who's living in a room in Soho. Monica shares the room with another woman. I dread to think how Monica's friend earns her living, but at least the baby is unaffected. He's got a cot behind a screen in the corner of the room. Everything is nice and clean. The place is visited regularly by a social worker.'

'When can I see the baby?' asked Joshua.

'Monica's bringing him up here at about tea-time this afternoon. If anything goes wrong, she'll ring. She's got a mobile phone.'

'Does Arthur look like you?' asked Joshua.

'No. He looks much more like you. He's fuller in the face than I am. Also, his hair is dark, like yours. The last time you and I saw each other, we were having lunch in Aunt Rita's house. What's happened to her?' asked Charles.

'She died quite some time ago,' said Joshua casually.

'You've broken the news of her death very abruptly. What did she die of?'

'An RTA.'

'RTA – what does that stand for? Is it some kind of gynaecological condition?'

'Joshua laughed, 'No. RTA means road traffic accident, you ninny!'

'I thought you were infatuated by her. How can you describe her death so coldly and without feeling?'

'Because my memory of her in life, as well as the knowledge that she is still there for me after her death, are so sacred to me that I lock them up,' said Joshua, who was being intensely economical with the truth. He added, 'That allows me to be outwardly cold when I think

87

about her. She lives within me now and the reminder that I've got her memory burning like a candle that never goes out, comforts me.' Joshua did not tell his brother about the heroine in his book whom he had decided to kill off in order to save his sanity.

'Do you really think that?' asked Charles.

'Yes. But I'm afraid there's another thing worrying me,' said Joshua.

'Oh, yes?'

'When I was with Rita once, I had some kind of fit. I saw a doctor who diagnosed epilepsy and who gave me some pills. He gave me three lots of pills – one for epilepsy, one for my anticipated psychotic episodes and some stimulants to keep me awake as the two other pills induced drowsiness which interfered with my writing. The stimulants are called Dexedrine. I prefer to refer to them as "running sweets" as a form of black comedy which comforts me.'

'So what?' asked Charles indifferently.

'The ones which keep me awake cause me to sleep fewer hours every night. I hear imaginary sounds. I get visual hallucinations. I get giggling fits. I shout at the walls. Perhaps there really is something wrong with my brain.'

'Come on, Joshua. I know you're one of the top nutters in the country. You've been like that all along. We knew things were going to get worse when our father was told about the MRI scan which was done when you were a baby,' said Charles.

'If you think I'm a nutter, how can you leave your son in my hands?'

'Because you seem to be caring, despite your nuttiness. Leave all the domestic work to a nanny. There's no way you can harm Arthur, because of your natural kindness. Just don't pick him up, that's all.'

'I've still got my books which sometimes take my mind out of myself,' said Joshua.

'How many books have you written?'

'Oh, several. Lord Brook-Owen has published the lot of them.'

'What's he like, Lord Brook-Owen?' asked Charles. 'He turned down all four of my books. I've only written four.'

'I don't know him very well. He took me out to lunch once. He's a pleasant enough man. My books are selling well.'

'Are you still writing bloodthirsty, dark, disturbing stuff with a lot of sex?'

'Of course I am. It's what the punters want, isn't it? You could have done the same, if only you'd stopped writing about espionage.'

'I haven't got your gift, Joshua. You write well. I write badly. That's all there is to it,' said Charles kindly.

'I wish you had said that when we were children,' said Joshua.

'So do I. I should have done. At least I'm saying it now,' said Charles. He smiled in a good-natured way at his brother, whose eyes had become dewy.

When Joshua went back to the Royal Free once more, he was afraid of being told that his brother had died.

Charles was still surrounded by wires and drips. On the bed, a horrifyingly skeletal woman was sitting, half dressed, with her arms covered with needle marks. Her real age was about twenty-five. She looked in her late sixties. She had been living in a sordid room in Soho, which she shared with a prostitute called Ruth. She was cradling a healthy, plump baby boy.

'Monica, this is my brother, Joshua,' said Charles, 'and this is my son, Arthur.'

'I've heard all about you,' said Monica. 'I'm so pleased you two have made it up. It's a terrible thing when brothers fall out.' She spoke with a pronounced Sloane

Ranger's accent. 'I understand you've very sweetly agreed to take Arthur in and look after him,' she added.

'I'm not doing so out of kindness,' said Joshua. 'I'm doing so because I've always wanted a son.'

Monica looked at Joshua.

'Do you know where Arthur's been living?' she asked.

'Yes. Charles told me he was being looked after by you and a lady living in a room in Soho,' said Joshua. 'He's a lovely-looking boy, isn't he? I'll wait until Charles is ready for his afternoon rest. Then I'd like to see your room. I'll carry the baby for you.' Joshua helped Monica to leave the hospital and held the baby. She could hardly stand up. They got into a crowded lift which took about twenty minutes to reach the ground floor.

'Why can't they treat you in this hospital?' asked Joshua.

'There aren't any beds,' replied Monica.

'That's terrible.'

'It *is* terrible. It's due to Tony Blair and his bloody New Labour.'

It took Monica, Joshua and Arthur forty-five minutes to reach the room where Arthur was being looked after by Monica and Ruth the prostitute. Joshua was even more impressed and ennobled by the red-cheeked, happy-looking baby which Monica laid in a cot and swaddled in a heap of clean blankets.

Joshua turned to Ruth who was taking a break from her activities on the streets.

'I say, it's most awfully kind of you to help look after my nephew like this, particularly as you've fallen on somewhat hard times,' he said thoughtlessly.

'Yes it is,' said Ruth, irritably. 'That brat's getting most of my meal ticket. The sooner he gets taken off our hands, the better.'

'I apologize on my friend's behalf,' said Monica. 'Ruth can be a hard woman at times.'

90

'There's no need to worry. Arthur's going to come home with me, once I've found a nanny,' said Joshua.

'How long will that take?' asked Monica.

'Not very long. It's just a case of advertising for a nanny and finally interviewing one who is suitable for the post.'

Joshua had a moody, sixty-five-year old neighbour called Mrs Lindle who had just moved next door to Rita's house. She had been widowed for three years and the only way in which she could assuage her grief was to sit by a bay window, doing tapestry. She liked rural scenes and covered her cushions with her work. In the summer, she sat on her lawn, sewing.

By the time she had moved into her new house, it seemed that Joshua's personal appearance had metamorphosed. His clothes were elegant and dapper, and he wore co-respondent shoes which he polished meticulously, as opposed to the soiled, white tracksuit he had worn before he had seen his brother in hospital.

Mrs Lindle disliked Joshua from the start of their acquaintance. She had often heard his clacking typewriter during the night through the thin walls of their houses. Joshua's bizarre habits grew worse. Sometimes, when he was in writer's block, he came out into the driveway, singing. When he was dissatisfied with his work, he crumpled papers into balls and threw them out of the window. If the winds were strong, the crumpled balls blew onto Mrs Lindle's lawn from Rita's garden.

Mrs Lindle did not have a sense of humour. She straightened out the paper balls and, out of curiosity, read them. On one occasion, when looking at a particularly ribald paper ball, she grew pale and staggered to a chair to recover from the shock.

The offending passage read:

Lucinda's aura was so electric that men within a twenty-foot radius of her had erections and longed to fuck her. She looked like a glorious goddess, from which concentrated sex oozed from every pore of her being.

Mrs Lindle thought of a way to approach Joshua and to use tactful language about the crumpled balls of discarded paper which had so greatly embarrassed and offended her.

She called on him at eleven-thirty one Saturday morning. He answered the door, wearing red pyjamas and a white bath towel dressing gown. On his pyjamas were embroidered his initials, J.F.

'I hope I haven't disturbed you,' Mrs Lindle said amicably.

'No. I sit up most nights, writing books, and I get up at ten o'clock. Was there something you wanted?'

Mrs Lindle took some crumpled paper balls out of a polythene bag.

'I understand these are yours,' she said.

'Yes, they are. Shall I say, they were. I threw them out. Why have you picked them up and brought them back to me? Hasn't it crossed your mind that your behaviour is a bit awry?'

'I straightened out some of the paper balls,' said Mrs Lindle disapprovingly.

'What the hell's the point of doing that?'

'I wanted to see the kind of things you write about.'

'I can't believe I'm hearing this, Mrs Lindle. If you want to buy my books, go to your local bookshop or get them on Amazon. Do you normally hang about, unravelling balls of paper discarded by writers?'

'I've straightened out some of the paper balls, as I said. I was struck by a particular passage. May I read it out?'

'If you must. I'm very busy. I've got three nannies to interview this afternoon, as my nephew is coming to live with me.'

Mrs Lindle straightened out about four of the paper balls before she found one which was particularly ribald. Joshua moved from one foot to the other and sighed loudly in frustration.

Mrs Lindle read aloud from the crumpled paper ball in a bizarre, theatrical voice.

'Oh, Mrs Lindle, if I wrote as badly as you read, I'd be the saddest man alive.'

'What sort of books are you writing, Mr Flinton?'

'Go to the shops. Look me up on the Net. My website address is www.joshuaflinton.net. If you haven't got a computer in your house, go to an internet lounge. That's a better method of research than wandering about, knocking on writers' doors.'

'I don't understand why you write this filth.'

'What you saw was discarded so what are you bothered about?'

'Does sex really play such an enormous part in all your books?'

'Go and see for yourself. If you want to know why lashings of sex and morbidity go into my books, it's because I've got to accommodate the black rubber mackintosh fraternity. They may be peculiar people but they're still a bloody fraternity, whose needs have to be catered for. I am a tradesman as well as a writer.'

'Could I just ask you not to throw your discarded pornography into my garden? My gardener is not among the black rubber mackintosh fraternity and he might find it offensive. He goes to church every Sunday. He's that kind of man.'

'So what?' said Joshua rudely.

'A devout man could easily be unhinged by your discarded paper balls. He might even lose his faith,' said Mrs Lindle.

'Oh, piss off, you silly old boot!' said Joshua.

Sometimes, Mrs Lindle looked over her other neighbour's fence to speak about Joshua's habits. 'He's a writer, you know. He's published several books and his name, Joshua Flinton, is known in bookshops all over the country. His late aunt Rita was a well-known concert pianist. Imagine that!'

Mrs Lindle was extremely snobbish. She liked to tell others who her famous neighbours were, even though Joshua's habits were unacceptable to her.

There was no change for the better in Joshua's behaviour. He often typed at a marble table on Rita's lawn in the summer, which interfered even more with the peace and quiet craved by Mrs Lindle.

She made herself tea to strengthen her nerves and tip-toed to her fence with her head bowed.

'Mr Flinton?' she called.

Joshua's typewriter continued to clack.

'...Er, Mr Flinton?'

Joshua pushed his carriage return and carried on typing. He was bending over his work with the look of a highly-strung jockey, and his eyes were glaring like a madman's.

'Mr Flinton, can you hear me?'

'Heard you but can't speak to you. Toddle off.'

'Look, Mr Flinton, if you don't stop making all that noise, I'm going to call the police.'

'If you did, they'd arrest you for wasting their time. Make yourself scarce. I'm busy.'

Joshua did not enjoy the prospect of interviewing nannies and did so with a heavy heart. He had asked an agency to send only old-fashioned, Norland nannies, to ensure Arthur's emotional security.

The first nanny arrived at two o'clock in the afternoon. She was too young for the post. She had a heavily made-up face, an orange leather mini-skirt and long black varnished nails.

Joshua let her in.

'You want a nanny, don't you?' said the woman casually. She spoke with a heavy Cockney accent.

'Go into the drawing room and sit down. I'll come in in a minute.'

Joshua went to the bathroom and looked at his reflection in the mirror. He could not control his maniacal drug-induced stare and he was astute enough to realize that his strange personality, which was induced partly by his abuse of the 'running sweets' which Dr Bennett continued to prescribe for him, had mutated. He put on a pair of dark glasses.

He went into the drawing room where the applicant was waiting, with her thighs exposed and her legs crossed. When Joshua looked her in the face, it was obvious that she was unnerved by his appearance.

'Do you want me to leave?' she asked.

Joshua was silent for a few moments. He bent over and untied and then tied up his shoelaces.

'I wish you hadn't come,' he said eventually. 'I told your agency I wanted a respectable-looking, mature lady to fill this post. You've wasted my time.'

She stared at him brazenly.

'That's too bad. Ever so sorry to have taken up your precious time!' she said in a sarcastic tone.

Two more nannies came to be interviewed. One of them was plump but had still kept her looks. She smelt of alcohol.

'You've been drinking,' said Joshua confrontationally. 'In fact, you've had quite a lot. Do you think I want a drunk looking after my nephew? You're the second woman who's wasted my bloody time. Bugger off!'

The woman eased herself to her feet, using the sides of her chair, and walked unsteadily towards the door.

'You don't realize how nerve-wracking it is, attending

interviews for jobs. Of course, I had a drink before I came here.'

'Not just one drink, three or four doubles, judging by the whiff of it,' said Joshua.

The third nanny to be interviewed was about sixty-five years old. She was a stereotype of a Norland nanny. Her name was Miss Marion McGregor. She had a strong Irish accent. She came from Dublin.

She asked serious and intelligent questions about the baby and the vacant job. She expressed a deep-rooted desire to work as a 'children's nurse'. It was her use of the words, 'children's nurse', which appealed to Joshua. The expression reminded him of glowing fires, hot buttered scones and apple trees.

'Have you got any references?' he asked politely.

'I've got two references here, if you would like to look at them.'

'I can already see you're suitable but I'll look at them all the same... Oh, just a couple more questions, Miss McGregor, before you leave?'

'Yes, sir?'

'Can you drive?'

'Yes, sir. I've got a Mini Clubman Estate. It's very reliable. It will help me to carry the cot, play pen, nappies etc., and all the other things the baby will need.'

'Do you believe in miracles, Miss McGregor?' asked Joshua.

'Oh, not really, except the ones described in the Bible.'

'I think your meeting with me just now is a miracle. I would love to appoint you.'

'I'm afraid I must insist on one thing, sir,' said Miss McGregor.

'Oh? What's that?'

'Your house is absolutely filthy, if I may say so, and your lawn needs mowing. I can't start working here until you've hired a cook, a cleaner and a gardener. When

Arthur is old enough to go to school, I shall insist that you appoint a woman who can sew as well.'

'Why a woman who can sew?' asked Joshua politely.

'To sew on the lad's name tapes, sir.'

'You certainly drive a hard bargain, Miss McGregor. I'll get a cook, a cleaner and a gardener, but, for obvious reasons, a woman who can sew will have to wait for at least five years.'

'When will you hire these members of staff?' asked Miss McGregor urgently.

'Give me two weeks. When can you start work?'

'Within that time. It will be an honour to work for you, sir. Are my references all right?'

'They are absolutely superb. When you begin work, how would you like to be addressed?'

'As "Nanny Marion", sir.'

Nanny Marion had been a spinster all her life. A suitor, who had been very kind to her and whom she adored, proposed to her when she was twenty-one years old. He wanted to have sex with his fiancée but Nanny Marion refused because she believed that sex before marriage was a sin. Her fiancé ditched her and broke her heart as she had always wanted children. She loved children.

'Nanny Marion,' exclaimed Joshua. 'What a cheerful, homely name! Now that the adoption papers have been finalized, I will ask the agency to supply a cook, a cleaner and a gardener. Then we will both be able to pick Arthur up from, well, where he's staying,' said Joshua, guardedly.

'Oh? Where is he staying?' asked Nanny Marion suspiciously.

'I'm afraid it's not much of a place as my brother is very poor. It's a relief that he finalized the adoption papers when he knew that he was dying. Arthur is the unwanted baby of my brother, Charles and his girlfriend, Monica.'

'Where is he staying, sir?' repeated Nanny Marion.

'In a room in Soho. It's warm and clean and the baby

is being taken care of, and is well looked after by Monica and her room-mate. We need to be there at twelve-thirty to meet the social worker.'

Joshua had no trouble hiring a cleaner, a cook and a gardener, because of the vast unemployment caused by the recession which was unaided by Tony Blair, followed by Gordon Brown. He and Nanny Marion took a taxi to be in time to pick up the baby. When they arrived in Soho, Nanny Marion instinctively knew that she was about to be taken to an insalubrious premises.

They arrived in Soho at a seedy-looking building in a back-street, bearing the words 'Massage Parlour' in neon lights.

Joshua sensed that Nanny Marion was beginning to regret her decision to accept the post.

'Oh, please, don't worry, Nanny Marion. It's only four flights of stairs up, and the baby boy has been receiving the best care that he can get so far,' he said nervously.

Once they had mounted the four flights of un-bannistered stairs, Nanny Marion sat down on the top step, gasping for air. Joshua was terrified that she was about to die on him, and dreaded the prospect of interviewing another batch of nannies.

'Oh, I say, Nanny Marion, are you all right? I did say it was only four flights of stairs,' he muttered tactlessly.

'Only? Only? If you ever ask me to go up four flights of stairs, again, I'll hand in my notice!'

'I'm so terribly sorry, Nanny Marion. I promise I won't ever put you through this again.'

'Kindly see to it that you don't, sir! Otherwise, you will be looking for another nanny.'

Joshua knocked harder than was necessary on the thin door leading to the room in which the baby was staying. The door crashed to the floor when he banged on it. The dust from underneath it looked like a rainbow in the ray of sun shining through the tiny window.

Arthur was lying in a cot, behind a screen, looking well fed. He was sparklingly clean and was flicking the different-coloured, plastic beads tied across his cot. A social worker was sitting down, baffled by the healthiness of the baby in his sordid surroundings. When she saw Joshua and Nanny Marion and spoke to them both at length, she was satisfied and said she was relieved to know that Arthur would be going to a good home. Monica was washing the baby's clothes and was friendly towards her visitors. Ruth was out working on the streets.

Joshua had already employed a cook, a cleaner and a gardener. The cook was middle-aged and even-tempered. The cleaner, though surly, did her work well. Nanny Marion was delighted by her new charge. Although she noticed something very strange about Joshua's mad, staring eyes caused by his abuse of 'running sweets', it would have broken her heart to be parted from the baby, just as the knowledge that Lucinda wasn't real had broken Joshua's heart.

In hot weather, Nanny Marion brought Arthur onto the lawn in a big black pram. She left him near the table at which Joshua was typing. The baby had a comforting effect on his uncle and lessened his frequent attacks of writer's block. He had reduced his dose of 'running sweets' at that time and was overjoyed by the fact that he had adopted his brother's son. However, he continued to appear extremely eccentric to those close to him.

Joshua had thought a lot about his brother since his last visit to the Royal Free Hospital. He had decided never to go back there, for fear of being told that he had died. His last conversation with Charles had been friendly and he did not want to spoil a memory which he wished to live with. The hospital would not have been able to write to him at Rita's address, as he had not left any details.

He was reasonably happy in the company of Arthur

and Nanny Marion. On some occasions, when he had attacks of mental illness brought on by the excessive use of his 'running sweets', as well as the insanity which his septicaemia had caused him, he blustered round the house and garden, singing. Many of the songs he sang were *risqué*. Others were mildly vulgar. Some were actually obscene. Nanny Marion tried to turn a blind ear to them.

When Joshua got into writer's block, these episodes were at their worst, and Nanny Marion locked herself and the baby in the nursery.

One of Joshua's songs was sung to the tune of *From Greenland's Icy Mountains*. The words of the song were:

> *Some dogs came to a meeting.*
> *They held it in a wood.*
> *They came to find some bitches,*
> *Because they thought they could,*
> *But bitches none they found there.*
> *The dogs got in a rage,*
> *And sodomized each other,*
> *So desperate by this stage.*

'Oh please, Mr Flinton dear, stop singing that ghastly, disgusting song,' pleaded Nanny Marion. 'I can hear it all the way from the nursery. Joshua ignored her and continued to sing.

> *The first dog's name was Brutus,*
> *Whose cock was made of steel.*
> *His partner's name was Rufus,*
> *Who could only yelp and squeal,*
> *And when their roles changed over,*
> *Things turned from bad to worse,*
> *For Rufus came too early,*
> *And Brutus turned off terse.*

100

Joshua stopped singing when he heard Nanny Marion crying.

Approximately ten years passed. Arthur looked like a clone of his uncle. He had an open-looking face and black hair. Both Charles's and the late Edward's hair were lighter, and their faces thinner. Joshua was still working on *The Killing of Lucinda Maloney*, but had written other books as well, all containing morbid, lurid and disturbing material, whenever he wanted to escape from *Lucinda*. In the summer, he continued to write at the marble table on the lawn. Arthur liked to read while his uncle worked and was comforted by the clacking of his typewriter. Joshua continued to smarten his appearance. He wore white trousers and an open-necked white shirt and a navy blue V-necked sweater most days. Further, the house was as clean as a new pin and the lawn was mown regularly.

It was an early autumn morning. The mists and the smell of bonfires had a saddening effect on Joshua, as he had always hated the autumn, because he associated it with going back to school where he had been bullied by older boys. He was working on *The Killing of Lucinda Maloney* once more, the book he had been tortured by for almost a decade. Even in his haste to finish it and believing that his heroine's death was imminent, his obsession about her worsened and ate into him like a cancer. He took the 'running sweets' which Dr Bennett had prescribed but not in quite such large doses as before.

Although he had decided to kill Lucinda, part of him wanted her to live and the conflict occupied him throughout his waking hours. There were times when he went to pubs to pick up red-headed women who reminded him of Rita and her brilliant, long red hair. Every time he failed to find his muse, he went to bed and limbless, black, slimy creature often visited him and crawled over his body. (He had no idea that this was only a hallucination.)

Joshua had thrown five balls of discarded paper onto the grass. Words were not coming easily to him that day, and Arthur sensed his discomfort. He went over to his uncle.

'May I have a look at those balls of paper, please?'

'No. Sorry. That would be out of the question.'

'Why?'

'Because you're only about ten years old. The books I write can only be read by adults. They would understand them but a boy of your age would not.'

'What are your books about?'

'About subjects which would bore you to death. What's that book I saw you reading just now?'

'*The Thirty Nine Steps* by John Buchan.'

'That's a very good book. Are you enjoying it?'

'Yes, it's all right.'

'What do you mean, it's all right? Have you not thought about the toil a writer goes through when he writes a book?'

'No. I haven't. Please tell me, what are your books really about?'

'Most of them are about cement.'

'Cement? That's awfully dull.'

'Yes, I know. That's why I told you that my books would bore you.'

The uncle and nephew came out onto the lawn again that afternoon. Joshua had severe writer's block. He had torn at least ten pages from his typewriter, rolled them into balls and and thrown them over his shoulder.

'Would you like me to take those into the house and put them into a wastepaper basket?' asked Arthur obligingly.

'It's nice of you to ask but they can be put to better use.'

102

'To what use?'

'Go up to the fence dividing our garden from Mrs Lindle's and throw them over it.'

'Won't that make her angry?'

'She deserves to be made angry.'

'Why?'

'Because she fails to give satisfaction, all round,' replied Joshua vaguely.

Arthur did as he was told. He always obeyed his uncle because his uncle was kind to him.

Mrs Lindle had aged dramatically over the previous ten years. Her gardener was off sick. She was kneeling down, gardening, when the first of ten paper balls landed on her head. The boy had not unravelled any of them because he assumed that his uncle had been writing an uninteresting book about cement.

'Was it you who threw that paper ball over my fence, Mr Flinton?' Mrs Lindle called out.

'No. It was me. I'm Mr Flinton's nephew,' said Arthur.

'Did your uncle tell you to throw it over my fence?'

'Yes.'

'Then tell him, the next time either of you throws a paper ball over my fence, I'll call the police.'

Arthur went over to the marble table and was surprised not to find his uncle typing. All he saw was the typewriter loaded with paper and a notebook and pen next to it. Only a few words had been typed on the paper.

Nanny Marion ran towards her charge, looking anxious and flustered, believing that the paper contained insalubrious material, unsuitable for the eyes of a child.

'Where's my uncle, Nanny Marion?' asked the boy.

'It would appear that your uncle hasn't been getting on too well with his writing this afternoon. I think he's in his bedroom.'

'What has he typed on that piece of paper?'

'Very little, my boy.'

Nanny Marion asked Arthur to come into the kitchen for his afternoon glass of milk.

'I'm going outside, Arthur. You stay here and drink your milk,' she said.

She went onto the lawn, scrutinized the document in the typewriter and was deeply upset by what she read. Some of the words were in capitals. Others were not.

I THINK I'M GOING INTO ONE. I'm going to my room. Just tell Arthur I'm not well.

Arthur was bored by Joshua's absence and went to his room. He took out pen and paper in an attempt to be a writer like his best-selling uncle. He thought this would be easy, as his uncle had managed to write so many books himself.

He sat on his bed. He had in front of him a large lined pad. The blank page, which had stared at him menacingly, chilled him. He had once been told that the most painful task facing an author was the writing of the first word. 'If you want to write a book, the easiest way to do so is to find a title first,' he was told by another acquaintance. The title, he was advised, would lead to the next worst hurdle, the first word.

Arthur looked at the blank paper for about ten minutes, by which time he had tears in his eyes. An hour and a half passed before his pen touched the paper. He had found a title.

LET'S PELT OLD WOMAN LINDLE

Another hour passed and he still couldn't think of the first word. He walked up and down in his room. It did not occur to him to look at the piece of paper in his uncle's typewriter on the lawn, because he assumed that his book was about cement. He felt like an examinee who had failed to revise.

Then, with a stupendous effort, his pen touched the paper once more. He summoned the courage to write the first word as if he were about to dive into a lake at the dead of winter.

The...

He had no idea what he was going to write next. He felt ashamed as he thought that he would be intellectually inferior to his uncle in later years and knew that, however much he tried, he would never be able to write a book.

He was stubborn, however, and he fought his disability.

He went outside and walked round the lawn. He returned abruptly to the piece of paper in his room, like a heavily constipated person who suddenly knows that he will defecate. He took up pen and paper for the second time.

The...

He waited, refusing to get up again. After about twenty minutes, he started writing.

The woman's name is Mrs Lindle. A fence divides our garden from hers.

He stopped again, and added,

Mrs Lindle sews all day long when she is not gardening. She is bad-tempered and does not get on with my uncle. She is boring because she is always bored. I do not like Mrs Lindle. My uncle does not like Mrs Lindle. In fact, I don't think anyone likes Mrs Lindle.

He was interrupted. He knew that he couldn't produce anything imaginative. He heard the fast flowing of water in the bathroom next door to his room and wondered why the bathroom was being used as early as three o'clock in the afternoon.

The water went on flowing for about ten minutes and gave the impression that its level was about to brim over.

Eventually, the taps were turned off. Arthur heard his uncle's footsteps crossing the bathroom to the basin. He cleaned his teeth and rinsed his mouth out over and over again. Although Arthur was intrigued, he thought his uncle's behaviour was disturbing and peculiar.

Joshua got into the bath and the water level cascaded onto the floor. The walls dividing the bathroom from Arthur's room were so thin that everything happening in the bathroom could be heard from the bedroom. Joshua clapped water onto himself several times over. He rubbed on soap and washed his body as well as his hair.

Instead of being satisfied that he was clean, he pulled out the plug and re-filled the bath. This time, he soaked the sponge with soap, repeated the procedure and washed his back with a loofah.

To Arthur's astonishment, his uncle let the water out and filled the bath a third time. He poured a bottle of Dettol into the bath and immersed himself in the water. He stood up, scooping the foul-smelling disinfected water over his body and slapped himself with the palm of his hand, making clapping noises once more.

Arthur was standing with his ear to the door, riveted. This was by no means the end of his bizarre uncle's ablutions. Joshua crossed the bathroom and turned on the shower, built with solid glass doors so as not to flood the bathroom.

Arthur heard his uncle go through the same process he had gone through when he was using the bath.

It was not until Joshua had been in the bathroom for over an hour that he stopped his washing ritual, and put on his bath-towel dressing gown.

He crossed the landing on his way to his bedroom. He found Nanny Marion, who was no longer a servant but a mother-figure. She was sitting at the end of his bed.

'Hullo, Nanny Marion. I'm so sorry about that. There are times when I can't exorcise whatever demon interferes with my writing. I have to wash myself over and over again to get the writer's block to go away.'

'Are you going about this in the right way, Mr Flinton, dear?' asked Nanny Marion mildly.

'How would you do it if you knew you were destined to become a world-famous writer?'

'I've got no idea what that feels like, Mr Flinton, dear, as I haven't got your wonderful brain. I suppose if I were trying to write something, even a postcard, I wouldn't force myself. I'd have a glass of cold milk and a biscuit or two, and wait until the words came to me.'

'Perhaps, perhaps...'

'How many baths have you had, today?' asked Nanny Marion.

'One before breakfast, one straight after breakfast, one before and after lunch, and one just now.'

'That makes four. How many more will you have today?'

'One before dinner, one just after dinner and one before bedtime.'

'That's seven in all, seven in one day. I'm so unhappy about all this, Mr Flinton, dear. The water tank here is big enough to fill a reservoir. You can have as many baths as you like, without depriving anyone of hot water. You know it's not that that I care about.'

'Does Arthur know about the baths? It would break my heart if he thought I was eccentric in any way,' said Joshua mildly.

'Your eccentricity isn't at all easy to cover up, is it, Mr Flinton, dear?' said Nanny Marion, adding, 'I'm sure he knows. He can hear the baths being filled. Have you spoken to him about it?'

'No. I want him to be happy. His happiness is even more important to me than my writing.'

'Oh, Mr Flinton, dear, what a saintly, kind-hearted man you are! There's no malice in you, at all. Your soul will go to Heaven, all right.'

Nanny Marion picked up a wet towel from the floor, folded it and put it on one of the radiators. Tears filled her eyes and rolled down her cheeks.

'How I wish I'd looked after you as a child, Mr Flinton, dear!' she exclaimed.

'Please don't cry on my account, Nanny Marion,' said Joshua. 'I'm happy most of the time, except when I get into writer's block. It's then that I have to wash myself like this, to stop the deadlock and the black blanket of slime crawling over my skin.'

Nanny Marion whitened in terror and disbelief.

'Oh, Lord, help my poor, tormented boss!' she muttered.

Joshua and Arthur had dinner with Nanny Marion that evening. Joshua did not look particularly distressed as he felt that the curse of deadlock had been lifted from him by his peculiar ablutions that day.

'You're a bit quiet, Arthur, my boy,' he observed.

'That's because I'm thinking.'

'Thinking, eh? Aren't you going to share your thoughts with your uncle and Nanny Marion?'

'I want to ask you something,' said the boy.

'Well, ask away. I'm listening.'

'Why do you have so many baths? Wouldn't one bath a day keep you clean enough?'

'You don't understand,' said Joshua. 'It may seem odd

to you, that I need to go through these rituals. I do so because the water somehow washes away writer's block.'

'How can it do that, Uncle Joshua?'

'Because I believe in it. Any ritual works if you believe in it. Do pass the grated cheese when you're finished with it. I'm hungry this evening. I think my bathing will do the trick and get my writing back to normal tomorrow.'

'Are you really writing a book about cement?'

'If I say I'm writing a book about cement, that means I'm writing a book about cement. Isn't that so, Nanny Marion?'

'Why yes, Mr Flinton, dear. A book about cement is a book about cement. No two ways about it. Come, along, Arthur, dear, fish fingers are not enough for a growing boy. You're to eat your green beans, potatoes and carrots as well.'

The next morning, Joshua felt more peaceful than he had the day before. There was a pleasant atmosphere in the house and garden. Arthur went out and sat in the chair near his uncle's table, and continued to read *The Thirty Nine Steps*. It interested him more than it had the day before and its robust, intriguing narrative occupied his mind, even more than his uncle's bizarre habits. It was not until an hour had passed that he felt his uncle's joy, shown in his radiant facial expression. He was typing fast and uninterruptedly and was laughing because he knew he was writing well, and at that moment was confident about the killing of Lucinda.

Joshua was engrossed in his heroine's sexuality, her long, red hair, her goddess-like beauty, her perfectly formed, silk-covered legs and even the soft, perfumed waft of air which seemed to sweep around her as she walked.

So strong was her presence, that he felt like tearing

the paper out of the typewriter. He wanted to hold her very being to his chest, as if by the mere action of keeping it close to his skin he could unfold it whenever he wanted to. He felt hand in hand with his muse and for one wonderful moment he convinced himself that she was not only real but immortal, like Rita.

Within seconds, his awareness of his need to kill her returned because she was too strong for him, however. He felt like an alcoholic looking at a bottle of whisky, yearning for it as well as being nauseated by it.

'How's your book about cement coming on, Uncle Joshua?' asked Arthur at dinner.

'Cement? Oh, yes, cement. I'm not having such a good run today. Where have you got to in *The Thirty Nine Steps*?'

'Oh, Hannay's managed to escape. I'm afraid the film's much better than the book. It shows Hannay, supporting himself on the outside of a moving train. When the going gets rough, he climbs into a compartment and kisses an unknown woman on the mouth in order to confuse his pursuers. I couldn't find that anywhere in the book.'

'It's an exciting book, all right, Arthur, my boy. You should read more books to occupy your time. It would help you to get out of yourself. One day, you may become a writer like your uncle and grandfather.'

'I get sad sometimes because none of all this dashing lifestyle affects our own lives,' said the boy. 'I'd like to escape from the real world and lead a fantasy life.'

Joshua felt a mixture of pride and sorrow. He was proud of his nephew, his sensitivity and his appreciation of the written word. He was also sad because of what he knew he had to do. He felt as if a cloud had suddenly covered a beautifully setting sun, and continued to be tormented until he cheered up during lunch the following day. He shovelled risotto into his mouth and spoke animatedly to his nephew.

'Artists, like writers, my boy, particularly the ones who paint, bring a sense of nobility and joy to those who survive them. Sometimes, a lot of writers resent artists and are jealous of them. A painter can splash up incomprehensible pictures which will be worth millions, and a brilliant writer might never be recognized.

'The writer's task is the hardest. We create three-dimensional people on a blank page. You must realize that I'm not in any way comparing myself with the great masters in the art world, as it is obvious that such painters as Botticelli and Caravaggio are more accomplished in their field than I am in mine,' said Joshua modestly.

Arthur thought for a while. He was ashamed of not having heard of Botticelli or Caravaggio.

'You told me that you got sad because you find some books more exciting than your own life. You said you wanted to escape from the real world and live in a fantasy world, didn't you, my boy?' said Joshua.

'Yes,' said Arthur, adding, 'that doesn't mean I don't like sitting on the lawn when you're typing. It's because I'm reading and am already in my own fantasy world. I like listening to you typing. It's when I'm indoors that I get sad. I want to be with the men in the few books that I have read.'

Joshua was reminded yet again of his own predicament and of a perfect character in his book, who could not be torn from the page and brought to life, and who therefore had to be killed. He spoke to his nephew as if he were talking to himself out loud.

'This is something you'll have to come to terms with, my boy. A book is only a book. It is there that you can create your own paradise and wander through pastures, which either you or the author has created. You can't do that in the outside world. You have to conform and do things against your will, sometimes, to accommodate others.' Joshua paused for a while and spoke once more. 'What happens if you fall in love with someone in a book? You'd be broken-hearted, because that person doesn't exist in real life. That's why I sometimes think books can be dangerous.'

The tormented writer wondered whether to confess the pain *Lucinda* was causing him and get it off his chest. He decided not to at first. He thought it would be unfair to impose his misery on a child. He hoped his nephew was still under the impression that his book was about cement.

'You look so sad, Uncle Joshua,' said the boy. 'I wish you'd tell me what's wrong. I'd understand.'

'I don't know if you would entirely, my boy. When I write, I often have trouble and when I'm not writing about cement, I write about something else. I write about a beautiful woman. I can't bear my heroine not being alive. It's something I've got to face, whether I like it or not.'

'But a book can live forever, though, just like art,' said the boy. 'Books written today will still exist centuries from now. We die but the books live on. Although you can't get the characters to come alive, they're immortal, unlike us. They'll still be active on paper when we're six foot under. Don't you think that's an optimistic thought?'

Joshua had not thought of that argument and was proud of his nephew's insight and intellect, way beyond his years.

'I've never thought of that, my boy. The best thing to do is to carry on and attain one's ambitions. We must try to conquer our sadness. Don't allow yourself to be invaded by dark thoughts such as mine. Be positive. You'll have to be quiet now as I've got to get on with my work.'

Joshua returned to his typewriter but found himself writing less fluently than he had earlier. He was feeling fortified by the bond between his nephew and himself, however. He had not realized before how much they had in common. Despite feeling a little stronger, he was haunted by the opinion he had expressed to the boy, as he was too disturbed to adhere to it himself.

Autumn turned to winter, and from winter to spring and finally from spring to summer. Arthur was about eleven years old. His presence gave Joshua the strength to believe that his decision to kill Lucinda was right. He did not realize until then how much he loved his nephew. Arthur filled him with gaiety and greatly relaxed him.

'Have you ever thought of writing books instead of just reading them, my boy?' Joshua asked Arthur who was sitting beside him on the lawn.

'I've tried, Uncle Joshua. You won't believe how much I've tried. I think you've got the gift in you but I have not.'

'Perhaps it will come to you when you get older. Your grandfather was a writer, as you know. He was similar to me in a way, except that he only wrote non-fiction whereas I adhere to fiction.'

Joshua turned away from his nephew and re-started his typing. The loud carriage returns made him feel that he and the red-haired Lucinda were frenziedly fornicating, just before her death.

'Uncle Joshua?' called Arthur.

'Yes. Just a minute. What is it?'

'It's weird old Mrs Lindle. She wants you to go to the fence.'

'Tell her best-selling authors are not accustomed to accepting summonses to fences.'

Arthur went up to the fence and repeated his uncle's words to the elderly widow.

'May I please come through into your garden, Mr Flinton?' called Mrs Lindle.

'No, I don't want you in here. I'll come over if you really want to speak to me. What is it?'

'Do you always have to use a typewriter outdoors?'

'Yes, I do. It's the summer. Perhaps you're not aware of that.'

'Why can't you write indoors?'

'Because it's more peaceful here, obviously.'

'For me, or for you?'

'For me. If you don't want to hear me typing, either go indoors or use some ear plugs.'

'Do you mind my asking if there is any history of mental illness in your family?' asked Mrs Lindle.

'Yes, I do. That was an appallingly impertinent question, Mrs Lindle.'

'I'm afraid your typewriter is disturbing my peace,' said Mrs Lindle.

'I've already told you what you can do.'

'All right. I'll tell you what I can do. I can sue you for breach of the peace and for being a noise pollutant.'

'Whose views do you think the Law will believe,' asked Joshua, 'the words of a best-selling writer, now a household name, or a whining, pestering woman who sews all day and contributes nothing to our national heritage? Your complaints are totally unreasonable. You have disturbed me when I've been writing before. If you did your sewing indoors, instead of on your lawn, you wouldn't be able to hear me at all.'

The argument between the two was circular and repetitive. Joshua enjoyed it at the beginning but became depressed as it continued. He felt that Mrs Lindle was interfering with the delicacy of his mission and was therefore endangering his health.

He picked up his typewriter and ream of papers and bundled them under his arm. Arthur followed him towards the house. Joshua noticed that Mrs Lindle was staring at him as if he were a Bedlam exhibit.

'What the hell are you staring at?' shouted the fiery, controversial writer.

Mrs Lindle continued to stare, as she held her tapestry and needle above the fence, and jabbed the air with her needle to give Joshua the impression that she was more menacing than he.

'The last thing I've got to say to you, Mrs Lindle is this,' said Joshua before he went indoors. 'You are not only disturbing me; you are upsetting my nephew and the smooth running of my household. If you continue to start unwanted conversations with me, I shall consult my solicitor and have you prosecuted.'

Joshua worked without interruption for the next two weeks and an aura of peace settled on his household. He was in the garden, typing. Arthur was sitting near him, reading. Joshua was three-quarters of the way through *The Killing of Lucinda Maloney* but he still felt as if his heroine were clinging to him like a limpet.

Joshua's work was suddenly interrupted by Nanny Marion. She was looking like the bearer of tragic news.

'Is there something the matter, Nanny Marion?'

'Oh, do come quickly, Mr Flinton, dear! There's a terrifying man at the front door.'

'Have you asked him who he is?'

'Yes, I have. He won't tell me. He's drunk. He's shouting his head off about his liver.'

'What do you mean, he's shouting his head off about his liver?'

'He says he has had what he called "a nice, fresh one fitted". He told me he wanted to speak to you, urgently.'

'Perhaps he's a canvasser for the Labour Party. Let him in and tell him to sit in the drawing room. He may be quite amusing. I might be able to put him in one of my books.'

'I'm afraid it's a lot worse than you think, Mr Flinton, dear. He's demanding to see Arthur.'

'Oh, he is, is he? I'll soon put a stop to that.'

Joshua went into the hall and pulled a heavy golf club

from its bag. He took it into the drawing room where the visitor was sitting. The visitor was bearded and was wearing frayed jeans and a dirty off-white T-shirt.

Joshua approached the man, brandishing the golf club. In comparison with his unwelcome guest, he looked immaculately neat and tidy. He was wearing a white shirt, a brown v-neck sweater and ironed white trousers.

'Who are you and what are you doing here?' he demanded.

'How can you ask me who I am? I am your brother, Charles. Don't you recognize me?'

'Charles! But I thought you'd ... gone. I was so upset, I couldn't bear to go to the hospital and be told you'd died.'

'I see. What sort of arrangements were you going to make for my funeral – you being my next of kin?'

Joshua felt like embracing his brother but he was too repressed to do so. Charles stared enviously at the pre-Raphaelite paintings on the walls in Rita's drawing room. Joshua had not made any changes to her interior decoration.

The brothers sat down awkwardly on a dark green, velvet-covered sofa. There was a pause of about five minutes, while they drank neat whisky. Joshua was the first to break the silence.

'I understand you want to see Arthur,' he said.

'Yes, I do. He's my natural son and I want him back.'

'You're mad! Don't you remember the signing of the adoption papers? He is legally under my care. Anyway, how could you possibly look after a child in your present state? Where are you living?'

'On and off at the Sally Army.'

'Do you mean the Salvation Army?'

'Yeah, that's about it.'

'What would you do with your son?'

'Send him to a state school, I suppose. Give him a bit of strength by training him to sleep rough, instead of letting him live here and be mollycoddled.' Charles refilled his glass with neat whisky.

'The last time we met, about eleven years ago, you said, to quote your own words, that you'd "smashed your liver". How have you managed to survive all this time?' asked Joshua.

'Had a transplant, didn't I?'

Arthur came into the room, accompanied by Nanny Marion. He was frightened by Charles's pungent odour and wild appearance.

'Who's he, Uncle Joshua?' he asked in a terrified, angry tone.

Joshua hated the situation he was in and wished he could continue with his writing.

'Oh, this is your father, my boy,' he eventually managed to mutter.

'What? Him? The man's absolutely filthy.'

Charles let out a stream of expletives. Some of the words he uttered were unknown to Nanny Marion.

Joshua was reminded of his childhood and the fact that it was his birthday. (The date was the twenty-second of June.) He often felt belittled and vulnerable on that day as his increased age had always made him self-conscious. He rose to his feet and shifted his weight from one foot to the other, as he always did when he was nervous.

'I am afraid I am not accustomed to being exposed to such utterly disgusting language on the twenty-second of June,' he muttered obscurely.

Arthur moved as close to his uncle as he could. He put one arm round his waist and sucked his thumb, his eyes wide open like those of an angel holding a lyre.

'I'm not going with him. I hate him,' he said.

'No one's saying you are going with him,' said Joshua. 'You are legally in my custody. Your father couldn't possibly look after you. He's a vagrant.'

Charles ignored the insulting description of him. 'Please, Joshua, I need help and only you can give it to me.'

'I'm not a bad person, Charles, and I never have been. I can see you're in need of money and I can start off by giving you a fifty-pound note,' said Joshua, adding, 'I've always felt guilty about the differences in our fortunes and to atone for that I'd like to offer you a weekly allowance, so that you can buy some decent clothes and find somewhere to live.'

'Do you really mean that? I don't deserve it. I was awful to you when we were children. Not only that, I was so nasty to you when we had lunch at Aunt Rita's that day.'

'That was then and this is now,' said Joshua kindly. 'I can offer you an allowance of eight hundred pounds a week. You can come here whenever you want, provided you behave and don't use foul language in front of Arthur and Nanny Marion. Your outburst just now was quite disgraceful. I can't have you living here, though, or staying overnight either.'

Charles felt ashamed of his behaviour in front of his brother, Nanny Marion and his son. He put on an act of coldness and aloofness to hide his guilt.

'OK. You'd better set up a bank account for me. I don't mean to sound ungrateful. It's not your fault that our fortunes have differed.'

Charles took the fifty-pound note from his brother. He crumbled it into a ball and stuffed it into one of his pockets.

'Thanks, little brother.'

'There's no need to thank me, but you will have to behave decently and refrain from rudeness and boorish behaviour, either towards me, Nanny Marion or Arthur when you are in this house. If you upset any of us, I shall stop your allowance and prevent you from coming here. All that I'm interested in is my writing, and Arthur's

118

'I don't think I'll settle into this kind of work,' said Joshua gloomily.

'You've got to. You'll get used to it. We're all trying to get *Lucinda* out of your head and our lives,' said Charles, adding, 'I'll tell you roughly what you'll have to do. You'll be with about five other people of mixed sexes. You'll be shown a moving screen which you'll be told to scrutinize. You'll be given plenty of breaks, so you won't get hypnotized or suffer from eyesight damage.

'Bottles of a probably revolting drink called Fizzipop will come by on a conveyor belt. If the bottles are orange, it means their contents are safe to drink. If they show up green, it means they're contaminated. If that happens, you press a button. That's all you have to do.'

'How do you know all this?' asked Joshua.

'The job centre rang me when you were in New York disgracing yourself. I said you had a stomach upset. You'll be accompanied by several factory workers, most of them permanent. I doubt if any of them will know about your escapade in New York. Only the *Daily Express* covered the story. I don't think many people working in factories read the *Daily Express*. It's a pretty conservative paper.

'I advise you strongly not to speak to anyone, unless you are spoken to first. You'd better disguise your accent. If you use your natural accent, the people in the factory will be likely to resent you,' said Charles.

'What's wrong with my natural accent?'

'It's a heavy public school accent, stupid.'

'What accent am I supposed to use?'

'Any accent you can mimic, but not Cockney. They'll see through that. What else can you do?'

'French.'

'Not a chance. When you speak with a French accent, you sound like a filthy old Arab, cleaning his teeth with a lavatory brush.'

151

'What about Welsh?' asked Joshua.

'That's possible. Let's hear you speak with a Welsh accent.'

Joshua uttered a few words with what he thought was a Welsh accent.

'No way, little brother. That sounds like a drunken Pakistani on a Saturday night.'

'I could try Irish?'

'Don't be crass. They'd call you "bomber boy".'

'American deep South. Listen to this.'

'You sound like a junkie trying to hold his bile.'

'I could try West Country.' Charles raised his eyebrows. Joshua mimicked the brogue.

'Full fathom five, my father lies. Of his bones be coral made. All my sheep got took sick in the night and died, God rest their blessed souls.'

'That's not too bad, little brother. You'll have to do some work on it, though. That's your best so far.'

'I'm so nervous. I've never had any real contact with the working classes before,' said Joshua.

'Don't be so bloody wet!' said Charles. 'Just do what everyone else does and button your lip. In other words, don't speak to anyone unless they speak to you first, as I've told you before.'

'I say, do these people not make any conversation when they're working?'

'Not dinner table conversation. They may talk about football, bingo, darts matches, the soap opera, *EastEnders* and not much else. If you have to speak, do so quietly and keep your eyes on the screen. If you don't, you might let green bottles go by and cause widespread poisoning. Your name would be given to your superiors and the job centre would cross you off its books.'

'I know this is going to take my mind off *Lucinda*, but I'm still nervous,' said Joshua.

'There's no need to be, little brother. You should be

pleased. For the first time in your life, you'll be thinking about other things and not just yourself.'

'Would it be considered odd to hum while I'm working? That's almost like speaking but without words.'

'I'm getting a bit bored with all this, Joshua,' said Charles. 'If they mind you doing that, they'll tell you. Keep the tunes politically correct. Any pop song or Russian folk song, if you like. I suppose *Molly Malone* would be reasonably harmless.'

'I'm good at Irish Rebel.'

'You'll be getting a good back-hander in a minute. Why don't you just toddle off and tumble into your cot? Even Nanny Marion, in the next door room, has overheard your fatuous questions. Isn't that so, Nanny Marion?'

Nanny Marion put her head round the door.

'I've heard quite a lot of them,' she said. 'Your younger brother can be ever so silly, particularly when he's tired. He's got no nous and at the same time he's a literary genius. The cleverer you are, the stupider you seem.'

'We're so lucky to have you living with us, Nanny Marion. You're part of our family now. You're about the only sane person here,' said Charles. 'Oh, except Arthur, of course, now that he's almost twenty years old.'

Joshua arrived at the factory at seven forty-five, the morning he was due to start work. He went through the front door and was faced by the word 'PERSONNEL' in capital letters on a cream-coloured wall which was covered with chipped paint. Underneath, in smaller letters, was the name Derek Bates, the Personnel Manager.

Joshua knocked timidly on the door. A loud male voice with a Yorkshire brogue called, 'Come in.'

'Good morning, sir. My name's Joss Flinton and I under-stand I'm covering for a gentleman with chicken-pox.'

'That's right, Joss. You're nice and early. My name's Derek Bates. Was your journey to work all right?'

'Yes, thank you, sir. I came by taxi, so as not to be late.'

'Good. It will be my colleague, Christopher Fable, who will be taking you down to the shop floor. He's one of our personnel officers. He's not in yet. I've just made coffee. Do you want some?'

'Yes. Milk and four sugars, please.'

'Sweet tooth, eh?'

'Er – yes, sir.'

'Have you worked in a factory before?'

'Unfortunately not, sir. I'm looking forward to the experience.'

'Don't call me, "sir"; call me "Derek". As you can see, this is quite a small factory, in comparison with others.'

Joshua sat down and drank some of the coffee which Bates had given him. Bates's friendliness put him at his ease.

'I hope you won't mind if I ask you a question,' said Bates.

'No, I don't mind.'

'Why have you come here dressed for a day at a golf course?'

'That's because I'm going to play golf at the close of business today. I'm sorry if my appearance confused you. Do you mind if I leave my golf clubs in the corner of your office?'

'Not at all. You'll be issued with protective clothing. As long as you do a good day's work, it doesn't matter what you wear underneath it. Even if you wore flashy, transvestite's lingerie under your working clothes, it wouldn't make any difference to production. There's just one other thing which I hope you won't mind my asking.'

'Not at all.'

'You've got ever such a strange accent. You're not

154

English, are you?'

'Yes, I am.'

'Have you lived in England all your life?'

'Yes. I was born in London and I went to school in London. I've spent the whole of my life in London, and I shall probably die in London.'

'What school did you go to?'

'Westminster School for Boys,' said Joshua shyly.

'There's no need to be nervous. I've got a fascination for different accents.'

Suddenly, a young man with centrally parted long dyed peroxide hair and disfiguring acne kicked open the door and dumped his briefcase on the nearest table.

'Joss, this is Christopher Fable, who's going to show you where you'll be working. Christopher's the fellow who makes all the noise.'

Joshua and Fable shook hands. Joshua was startled by Fable's extremely limp handshake and took an insant dislike to him.

Fable made himself some black coffee and drank it so quickly that it was clear from the expression on his face that he had burnt his tongue.

'Have you brought your time-sheet along with you, Joss?' he asked.

'Yes. The job centre left it with my brother. I'm not quite sure how to use it.'

'It's very simple,' said Fable. 'All you have to do is fill in the hours you work every day, except for the lunch hour. The hours are eight o'clock until four o'clock. You can take your lunch break from midday till one o'clock or from one o'clock till two o'clock. There's a canteen on the third floor.'

'Is it licensed?' asked Joshua. There was a slight note of urgency in his voice.

Fable and Bates laughed. 'No, it isn't,' said Bates.

155

'Alcohol slows down production and causes our staff to make mistakes. Christopher, would you please take Joss next door and issue him with some protective clothing.'

Fable and Joshua went next door.

'Why are you dressed in golfing clothes?' asked Fable, his tone fractionally unpleasant.

'I've just been talking to Derek about this. I like to play a few holes after work, to unwind.'

'Is that so? Of course, there are no regulations about the clothing you wear under your overalls. Are those your golf clubs in Derek's office?'

'Yes.'

'Did he say you could leave them there?'

'Yes. Yes, he did.'

'Come on, I'll take you down,' said the other man abruptly.

Joshua was unnerved by Fable's manner. His thoughts returned painfully to the killing of Lucinda. He thought briefly about her sexuality, which caused him to feel a combination of pleasure and pain. He held one of the bannister rails tightly, as he suddenly felt faint.

'Are you all right, mate?' asked Fable.

'Yes, I'm OK.'

'Your face is white. You look upset. What's the matter?'

'There's nothing the matter.'

'Yes, there is, mate. Are you in some kind of trouble?'

'Oh, no!'

Fable repeated the words, 'Oh, no,' mimicking Joshua's upper class accent. Joshua felt a sudden gush of Lucinda's physical and mystic presence, contrasting with his need to kill her. The sensation was like a burning furnace and a Siberian wind blowing into his face at the same time.

'You look bloody done in, mate. Bad hangover, eh?'

'When I tell you there's nothing wrong with me, that is not a euphemism for saying there's something wrong.

I mean what I say. There is nothing wrong. If there were, I'd say so.'

'OK, mate. Contrary to my questions, I'm not really interested in whether there's anything wrong with you or not. I've been given orders to take you down to the shop floor so that's what I'm doing.'

'I personally think there's something wrong with *you*,' said Joshua unwisely.

'Like what?' asked Fable aggressively.

'You're very abrupt. Have you taken a lot of other factory staff down to their place of work?'

''Course I have, stupid! I've been here for two years, haven't I?'

'The people you took down, did they say your manner was somewhat terse?'

"Can't remember. I don't really care. I'm getting out of here as soon as I find another job.'

'Are you looking for any situation in particular?' asked Joshua, only to make polite conversation, in contrast to his previous answers to Fable's questions.

'M.Y.O. bleeding B!' replied Fable.

Five workers, three of them women and two of them men, were sitting motionless, in front of a mesmerizing screen. Brian Taylor, their supervisor, wasn't there. An unending array of bottles was moving from one end of the screen to another. They showed an orange drink. The appearance of the bottles nauseated Joshua.

Fable introduced him to the other factory workers and told him what his duties would be. The first thing which struck Joshua was the powerfully hypnotic experience he would have, if he stared at the screen without taking a break. It meant that he could obliterate *Lucinda* from his thoughts during his working hours. The thought cheered him up and he felt a slight surge of mania, even though he had forgotten to take his 'running sweets' that morning.

None of his fellow-workers spoke to him or even smiled at him. Joshua wanted to gain their attention and hopefully, their affection.

His eyes had been fixed on the moving bottles and were glazed, like those of many people going through mania.

'I say,' he began in a startling tone, without bothering to cover up his public school accent, and stubbornly ignoring his brother's words, 'are any of you chaps into Russian literature?'

No one answered him. The thought crossed Joshua's mind that his fellow workers were foreign and did not speak English.

'I say, does anyone here speak English?'

The same thing happened. Joshua thought at first that someone would have answered him. He continued to look at the screen. He thought he could see a tunnel, suggestive of his tunnelled vision at the centre of his obsessive compulsive disorder. He started speaking once more.

'I say, I strongly recommend Max Gorki's works. He's dead now. He was Russian and he was a commie. He was amazingly into the factory workers' scene. The workers he describes weren't like any of you. They were much noisier. They liked to shout about the grimness of their working lives. Frequently, they dropped dead on the job. Old Max didn't like a whole lot of people bumbling about. Big numbers confused him. That's why he liked to bump his protagonists off early. They often reappeared in the next chapter because he'd forgotten he'd done away with them.'

Joshua was astounded by the fact that no one commented on his lively chatter.

'I say, here's one which might challenge you. It's a question addressed to the ladies here. I don't know whether or not any of you have read Dostoevsky's novel, *Crime and Punishment*. If you have, do you ever get fantasies

158

about being fucked by Raskolnikov on the floor of his garret?'

One of the men stared at Joshua, as if he had swallowed a wasp. Joshua tried to moderate the tone of his conversation.

'I say, does anyone here take *The Daily Worker?*'

Joshua was becoming convinced that his audience consisted of non-English-speaking foreigners but his compulsive mania took hold of him.

'Perhaps, your silence means, "No". I'm surprised no one here takes *The Daily Worker*. It always refers to the misery of working people's lives.'

Joshua was silent for about ten minutes. A sobering thought passed through his mind. Just as he was suffering because he had created a fictitious woman whom he couldn't kill, he remembered that Flaubert had had a nervous breakdown when he was writing *Madame Bovary*. He had actually stated, 'I *am* Madame Bovary.' The confession made Joshua shudder, because he feared that Lucinda would live within him for the rest of his life.

He ignored the presence of the silent workers and in his ongoing mania, he suddenly wanted to shout with joy, to tell anyone who could hear him that he was concerned about another person's suffering, instead of thinking about his own pain.

'I say, does anyone here know about that nervous break-down Flaubert had, when he was writing *Madame Bovary?*'

The lack of response made Joshua angry. He raised his voice.

'I say, doesn't anyone here care about Flaubert's suffering? Or about the pain endured by sensitive writers? Don't you fellows ever read anything? Do books mean nothing to you?'

There was a long, uncomfortable silence. One of the workers turned away from the screen and faced Joshua.

He was a stooped, staring, red-eyed man, who was about forty years old although he looked at least sixty-five years old. Although his mother language was English, he failed to understand a word Joshua was saying.

His face broke into a smile. His teeth were dark brown. Many of them were missing. His only care was the availability of his next bottle of methylated spirits.

'I say, sir, oh, I mean comrade, you really do look like someone straight from the pages of dear old Max Gorki,' said Joshua insensitively. 'There is something uplifting about your run-down appearance if I may say so.'

The man walked towards Joshua. His gait was so slow that his motion and station seemed as one. As he walked, he stared at Joshua's eyes. Joshua longed for him to speak, if only to form a relationship with another person, to take his mind off his obsession.

'Oh, God, I'm just wracked by obsessions!' he said, his voice raised.

'Oh, aye? I'm obsessed by racks,' said the man half-wittedly.

'I'm so lonely. I only want someone to talk to. Don't you ever read anything? Have you got no knowledge of Madame Bovary's mental pain?'

The meths drinker smiled more broadly. Joshua was filled with hope as he watched him move closer to him. He opened his mouth and was about to speak.

'Yes?' said Joshua.

The man allowed his head to tilt to one side.

'Roll on me pench!' was all he was able to mutter.

'I say, I don't understand why none of you are willing to make conversation. You may think my accent's a bit awry but that does not mean I'm rich or privileged. I've got to scrape the bottom of the barrel,' Joshua lied, adding, 'you just don't understand – I've always tried to get along with the working classes because of their struggle against capitalism. So terrible is this recession that at least a third of the nation is unemployed. We destitute folk are forced to take jobs like these. If we didn't, we'd starve.'

Joshua felt another gush of mania surge through him, as if he had just taken his 'running sweets'. 'And it's all going to get worse, worse, do you understand, not better? I know it in my bones. The bleeding sons of Jarrow shall throng our streets once more! Dying mothers shall lie swaddled in doorways, their emaciated babies sucking their empty breasts. England is already a third-world country.'

All Joshua wanted was to be liked by his colleagues and be regarded as one of them. He could not bear rejection, even from strangers. He still failed to adhere to Charles's advice not to speak to anyone unless spoken to first.

'I say, don't you know what Lenin said in his manifesto? He said, "We'll build gold latrines for the workers". How compassionate of him, how kind, how thoughtful! I'm afraid I was disappointed by Leninism. I had a horrible shock. I went to the lavatory in East Berlin once, expecting it to be made of solid gold, and when I pulled the chain, the ballcock came away in my hand and the cistern crashed to the floor.'

'Oh, naff off, you crappy old toff!' muttered the meths drinker.

Joshua stayed on the shop floor but gave up his efforts to make conversation with his fellow workers. He sat in silence, looking at the passing bottles, until it was time to go home.

At four o'clock, he went to pick up his golf clubs from Derek Bates's office. Bates touched him gently on the shoulder.

'Christopher's gone home. I'll sign your time sheet for you, Joss.'

'Shouldn't that happen on Friday afternoon?'

'I'm afraid not, not in your case. You can't come back tomorrow.'

'Why not?'

'Well, er, I don't want to be rude, because you seem to be such a nice person.'

'Indeed?'

'The truth is you had an awfully traumatic effect on the shop floor staff. You don't relate to people in an appropriate manner.'

'What do you mean? To whom have I not related in an appropriate manner?'

'Well, I don't claim to be much of a scholar and I have nothing against those who are, but you terrified those people by shouting about Russian literature, namely the works of a certain Max Gorki and Dostoevsky, and a French lady, whom I assume is a friend of yours, called Madame Bovary. When one works in a factory, one doesn't sit there shouting about people totally unknown to the staff. You were interfering with their concentration.'

'I was only making polite conversation. Isn't that allowed in the workplace?' said Joshua.

Mivart Jones, the shop steward, a short, but good-looking Welshman in braces, came into the office and made himself tea.

'You haven't met Joss Flinton, have you?' said Bates. 'Joss, this is Mivart. He's our shop steward. Joss has worked here for the day. He'll be going somewhere else, tomorrow, I should imagine.'

Jones stared at Joshua.

'Is your surname really Flinton?' asked the Welshman.

'Yes.'

'Your first name's Joshua, isn't it?'

'That's right.'

'You're Joshua Flinton, the writer, aren't you? I recognize

162

you. You look like the photograph on the back covers of your books.'

'Well, I never!' said Joshua modestly.

'I'm so sorry you're not coming back tomorrow. I would have liked to talk to you about your books. They're fascinating. Would you mind giving me your autograph? Then I can glue it into one of your books.'

Jones handed a pen and a piece of paper to Joshua who had become slightly emotional. His eyes filled with tears. He would have loved to work in the same place the following day and was hurt when he was told that he was not required. At least Jones seemed glad to have met him. Joshua's hands were shaking. He could hardly hold the pen to sign his autograph.

'Come on, Mr Flinton,' said Jones. 'This would be such an honour.'

Joshua signed his name, his hands still shaking.

'Would you like to come and play golf with me?' he asked, after a pause.

'I'm afraid I can't play but I'll never forget that a best-selling writer invited me to.'

'It's time for both of you to go home,' said Bates. He sounded tired and bored.

Joshua was surprised to see Charles standing by the factory gates.

'Charles!'

'I'll hand it to you that at least you tried to put in a hard work,' said the elder brother, somewhat coldly, adding, 'even though they don't want you to come back tomorrow.'

'How do you know they don't want me to come back tomorrow?' asked Joshua.

'They've got my number. The personnel manager rang me up and told me about your earth-shattering behaviour. You banged on about Flanbert, Gorki and *fucking* Dostoesky. You really are a certified raving basket case! I thought I told you not to speak to anyone unless they spoke to you first.'

It was sunny the next morning. Joshua, Charles, Nanny Marion and Arthur were eating bacon and eggs and drinking coffee in the kitchen. Arthur had prepared the meal. He was as concerned about Joshua as Charles was. Both were worried that he might start writing in the privacy of his room, unless his typewriter were confiscated.

'I was thinking we might go for a walk on Hampstead Heath this morning. Then we could go to the West End and see a film,' suggested Charles. 'What do you think, Nanny Marion?'

'What a nice idea! Mind you, a lot depends on the kind of film we'll be seeing.'

'What about *The Sound of Music*?' asked Arthur. 'That's listed in the *Evening Standard*.'

'I think we've all seen it before, haven't we?' said Charles.

'I haven't seen it for quite a few years,' said Joshua. 'I don't mind seeing it again. What will happen if my mobile phone rings during the film and the job centre wants me to work again?'

'It's very important to maintain professional discipline. If they want you, you go straight away,' said Charles, 'whether you've been interrupted during the film or not.'

The family went for a long walk on Hampstead Heath and, despite the late frosty autumn weather, they had a picnic lunch before going to London's West End by bus. *The Sound of Music* had been listed in the *Evening Standard* as being shown at the Odeon, Leicester Square. It was alleged to have made a come-back. When the family got there, they found out that the film *Jude*, based on Thomas Hardy's *Jude the Obscure*, was showing instead.

Charles got into a heated argument with the man issuing

tickets, and thrust the *Evening Standard* in front of him, showing a ring round *The Sound of Music*. The man repeated several times that this wasn't his fault. Charles sent for the manager and a heated row blew up between the two of them.

'I can't bear scenes,' exclaimed Nanny Marion, in a distressed tone. 'Why can't we see the new film, anyway?'

'OK, Nanny Marion. *Jude* happens to be on. I suppose we can see that instead,' said Charles abruptly. (He knew nothing about the disturbing contents of the film.)

The family found the first part of the film mildly entertaining, but became despondent as it progressed, with the exception of Joshua who appeared to be stimulated by it. Nanny Marion, however, found it profoundly depressing. She spoke out loud, across a stranger, sitting between her and Charles. Joshua was sitting on Charles's other side.

'Oh, Mr Charles, I don't think this film is good for poor Mr Flinton's nerves. Are you all right, Mr Flinton, dear?'

'Yes, thank you, quite all right. I'm over twenty-one, Nanny Marion,' replied Joshua almost rudely.

The film had reached the scene in which Arabella's son, a plump, unprepossessing-looking boy, strangles his half-siblings, before hanging himself, and leaving a pathetic note saying 'DONE BECAUSE WE ARE TOO MENNY', the words being more disturbing, because of the misspelling of the word 'many', than because of the heinous deed they related to.

It was too much for Nanny Marion. She sobbed convulsively, and between sobs called out, 'Oh, Mr Flinton, dear, is this upsetting you? You've only got to tell me.' The occupants of the row in front gesticulated and hissed. The brothers were mortified with embarrassment.

'For God's sake, cool it, Nanny Marion! How could the film possibly be upsetting Joshua, who's only interested in ribald books about buxom redheads copulating?' said Charles. 'You know perfectly well, he's not upset by the notion of ugly boys strangling their half siblings before topping themselves.'

A middle-aged man in the row in front of the family turned round and fixed Charles and Nanny Marion with a furious stare. He hit Charles on the head with a rolled up copy of the *Financial Times.*

Joshua's mobile phone rang. He could hardly hear what was being said because of the loud sobbing coming from most members of the audience.

'I can't hear you, blast it! I just can't hear you! So you want me to do some photocopying for a firm of solicitors in the West End? Who do you want me to report to? Who? I still can't hear you!'

The caller asked Joshua where he was.

'I'm in a bloody cinema in Leicester Square, blast it! Everyone around me is sobbing their guts out! You still haven't told me. Who the hell do I report to? ... Mr Who? What?'

Charles reached out and grabbed hold of Joshua.

'Come on, little brother, out of this fucking cinema, now!'

'Language, Mr Charles!' exclaimed Nanny Marion.

Charles dragged his brother outside into Leicester Square. The details of Joshua's next assignment were given to him. He wrote them down on the palm of his left hand.

'I'm nervous, Charles, particularly after what happened, yesterday,' said Joshua.

'You're going to behave this time, little brother. You're going to keep that fucking mouth of yours shut and in no circumstances are you going to talk to anyone about bloody Russian literature, or any other subject!'

'I promise I won't.'

'That's good, because if you do, I'm going to give you a good crack.'

Joshua got on well with his colleagues in the offices of the West End solicitors. They were situated in Jermyn Street. He did his work efficiently and went out of his way to be polite to everyone he met. He took his brother's advice and never spoke unless he was spoken to. The women on the premises thought he was unusually shy and were attracted by his pleasant facial expression and dapper appearance.

A typist had also taken a liking to Joshua and his gentle, quiet mien. She approached him one morning.

'Come on, Joss, when are you going to take one of us girls out for a drink? she asked.

Joshua invited all the women out at once and bought them drinks in a nearby pub during the lunch hour one day. They competed for his attention. One of them, a slim, Cockney brunette in her early twenties, sensed his discomfort.

'Oh, it's all right. We all know how you feel. You're shy, that's all but you're a gentleman in every sense of the word,' said the brunette kindly.

'Oh, no, I hardly think...'

'Course you are! What do you like doing when you're not at work?'

Joshua could hear Charles's voice, 'Don't talk about bloody Russian literature or *Lucinda* either, if you know what's good for you, little brother!'

'I'm afraid I haven't got very many hobbies but I do like going for long walks,' said Joshua, his head bowed like the bearer of sad news.

Joshua worked in the same place for over six months and was reasonably happy there. He was temporarily relieved of his obsession about *Lucinda*.

His happiness at the firm came to a halt, however. A change in management caused his misery to return. The women continued to be nice to Joshua and shared his hatred of the new managing director, Sebastian Fentwood. He was a very slight man with dyed black hair cut in a short back and sides. The fact that the firm was not unionized made working conditions unpleasant and the atmosphere strained and uncomfortable. The staff grew neurotic and paranoid.

Since Fentwood had replaced the good-natured, easy-going, Henry Hills, his former boss, Joshua foresaw that he would probably be dismissed and that he would have no alternative but to go home to his mental prison, where his typewriter (his lethal liquor) would drag him towards it like a magnet, before he was ready to kill Lucinda.

He made sure that he arrived at the offices a quarter of an hour early every morning, only took fifteen minutes for lunch and left ten minutes after closing time.

One morning, Fentwood summoned him over the antiquated tannoy system.

'Get over to my office, Flinton I want to see you, now,' he said peremptorily.

Joshua knocked timidly on the door, waited to be told to come in and stood in front of Fentwood's desk, with his hands clasped in front of him and his head lowered.

'You wanted to see me, sir,' he said quietly.

'Yes. I've decided to take you off photocopying duties, now. Since the workload has increased, we are having volunteers in to photocopy documents. We're putting you in charge of the metal strips which should correspond with our clients' files.'

Fentwood leant over and picked up three boxes, so full of cramped metal strips that it was uncomfortable for anyone to handle them.

'The names in these three boxes are not in alphabetical order,' said Fentwood. 'It will be your duty to take them out and arrange them in alphabetical order. When you've completed this task, you will arrange the clients' files in alphabetical order as well and clip the metal strips onto them. You may not have seen a client's file. If you haven't, I'll show you what it looks like.'

Fentwood pointed to a thick, beige file which was lying on his desk.

'The files are in the cupboard in the corridor and they are equally as tight-fitting as the metal strips. You may consider this an undesirable task,' he said, adding, 'many people have already. I've had to dismiss them. If you're prepared to do this work, you might get the occasional perk. If you do not wish to comply, you will be dismissed, just as unwilling staff members have been dismissed before. What do you say?'

'I would like to do my very best, sir. I shall do as you ask.'

'Good. I note with satisfaction that not a single complaint has been made about you since you first started to work here six months ago. This is most laudable.'

'Thank you, sir. I am here to serve. I like doing what I am told to do and doing it well.'

'Good, Flinton. I'm sure we shall be friends.'

'As a humble office clerk, sir, I am most proud and honoured to be at the receiving end of an offer of friendship from a gentleman of your rank,' muttered Joshua sycophantically.

Fentwood leant back in his swivel chair and laughed.

'Do you know what I find so charming about you, Flinton?'

'No, sir.'

'It's not only your work ethic attitude. It is your speech mode which I find enchanting. You're so old-fashioned. You're like some of those sweet, old-fashioned servants we sometimes see on television. You remind me very much of that man, Hudson, in *Upstairs Downstairs*, which is about Edwardians as you are probably aware.'

Someone knocked on the door.

'That will be the old bag, bringing in my elevenses. All right, come in.'

Joshua opened the door for her. The serving woman had worked for the firm for twenty-five years and had been loyal, even when Fentwood took over.

'For God's sake, you half-witted woman! What time does one have one's elevenses?' shouted Fentwood.

'I'm so sorry. Eleven o'clock, sir.'

'What time do you think it is now?'

'According to my watch, it is nine forty-five, sir.'

'Does that mean that nine forty-five and eleven o'clock are the same time?' asked Fentwood rudely.

'No, sir. I apologize, sir.'

'All right. I'm prepared to forgive your stupidity on this occasion. The next time you do anything like this, I shall dismiss you. Do you understand?'

'Yes, sir.'

The woman was called Agnes Johnson. She was heart-broken because she had recently been widowed. She was overweight, grey-haired and prematurely aged. She took the tray outside and burst into tears. On the tray was a pot of Indian tea, chocolate biscuits, arranged neatly on a doily'ed plate, a jug of cold milk and white sugar cubes, topped with sugar tongs.

Fentwood and Joshua were alone.

'I do wish you'd sit down, Flinton. It's most unnerving when I'm sitting while someone else is standing.'

'Oh, sorry, sir.'

'There's something I wish to tell you.'

'Sir?'

'The brain chemistry between us appears to be quite unusual. In future, I'd like you to address me as "Sebastian" and, if I may, I would like to know you as "Joshua".'

'I'm glad you seem to like me, Sebastian. I'm only a

lowly man and I've got few social graces. I hope our association will not be a disappointment to you.'

'Although I abhor arrogance in a young man, self-deprecation is slightly irritating in a different way,' said Fentwood. 'You are more noble in mien than you think. You do not see yourself as others see you. It's a shame that men of your modest, hard-working kind are so rare. It's like seeing an emerald in a basin of offal.'

Joshua laughed politely. 'I've been compared to many things but I think the word "emerald" is a trifle strong,' he said modestly.

'Bless you for that spontaneous witticism! Tell me, what do you do when you're not at work?'

'Nothing of great worth, Sebastian. I live with my brother, Charles, his son, Arthur, and an old nanny, who is alone in the world, and who has become one of the family.'

'I take it, the nanny looks after Arthur, as opposed to you?'

Joshua laughed again but did not say anything.

'What does Charles do?'

'He's retired now. He was terribly ill quite some years ago and nearly died.'

'Is he in good health, now?'

'Yes, thank you.'

'What does he do with his time, I just asked you?'

'Not an awful lot. Sometimes, he reads Ian Fleming's books. He's the only author he likes.'

'I quite like Ian Fleming,' said Fentwood. 'He's a good read if you're not feeling very well. He bounces along but I do think all this gadgetry is very tedious and silly. The idea of a man in a black bow tie, darting about with a Smith & Wesson in each hand, is rather ludicrous.'

'I agree. I'm not much of a reader of Ian Fleming's books,' said Joshua.

'You must have some interests. You're gentle and sensitive.

171

You don't strike me as being a man who watches *EastEnders*, attends football matches and has nights out with the lads. You seem shy and quiet. Come on, tell me what you like doing?'

Joshua would almost have torn off his fingernails to keep the approval of Fentwood, so that he could postpone the work he adored but which was also an anathema to him. Were he to be drawn into it too early, he feared he would never exorcise his demons and would spend the rest of his life in a mental institution.

'I'm afraid I'm what would have been described as a bit of a "square", to quote the slang words of the nineteen-fifties,' replied Joshua after some thought.

'Do you mean by that that you go to church on Sundays?'

'No. What I like doing most is going to my favourite golf course after work in the summer and at weekends. I play a few holes and I feel a different person.'

Fentwood leant forward in his chair.

'Which golf course do you go to?' he asked.

'Gadmartin. It's on the outskirts of north London.'

'Never!'

'Yes, that's right. Gadmartin.'

'This is an extraordinary coincidence! That's where I go. We probably bumped into each other before I took over the firm. Do you play at weekends as well as weekdays?'

'I like to play during all my spare time, if I can.'

'How would you like to have a game with me on Saturday?' asked Fentwood. 'I've got a lot of free time on my hands. I haven't got any children to occupy myself with and my wife divorced me a few years ago. It doesn't worry me, though. I prefer living alone.'

'I'd very much like to play golf with you on Saturday,' said Joshua reluctantly.

'Good. Shall we meet at the course?'

'Yes, that would be easier. What time's convenient for you?'

'Is ten-thirty all right with you?'

'Yes, it's perfect.'

Joshua worked like a navvy and got a quarter of the way through the metal strips in the first box. The boxes containing them were so tight that he cut the tips of his fingers, particularly when he put the strips back. He took care to keep them rigidly in alphabetical order.

It was four-thirty on a Friday afternoon. Fentwood left his office and found Joshua, who was on his knees, slaving in a tiny, overheated, windowless office.

'How have you been getting on, Joshua? Let's see what you've done.'

'I'm only a quarter of the way through the first box, I'm afraid. I'm working as fast as I can. The strips are in strict alphabetical order, so far, Sebastian.'

'Splendid! You've covered a lot of ground. Congratulations!' Suddenly, Fentwood looked concerned. 'There's blood on the strips you've just arranged, Joshua.'

'I'm so sorry. I tried to stop getting blood on them. The metal corners are like razors.'

'I can see blood all over your fingers as well.'

'Once I've finished the first box, I'll wash it off with a nail brush.'

'You are so self-sacrificing and dedicated. I'm ashamed of the somewhat abrupt way I spoke to you, when we first met.'

'Come on, Sebastian, life's too short to be ashamed. If I didn't like working for you, I'd leave,' said Joshua cordially.

Fentwood and Joshua kept their appointment at the golf course. Joshua wore conventional golfing clothes, namely tweed plus-fours, a red sweater and matching red socks, but Fentwood looked slovenly. He was wearing a shabby, pale blue tracksuit which accentuated his dyed black hair and made him look comical.

It was then that Joshua noticed how short his companion was in comparison with him. His boss was only five foot tall, nearly a foot shorter than he was. It occurred to Joshua that Fentwood might have had a complex about his height and to compensate for this bullied his underlings with Napoleonic arrogance.

The two men went out onto the green.

'Why don't you play first, Sebastian?' ventured Joshua timidly.

Fentwood knew that Joshua was secretly laughing about his shortness. He smiled at him to hide his resentment.

He bent over, placed his ball on top of the tee and put every ounce of energy into his swing. His movement was so violent that his whole body circled round and he faced the same direction he had started in without touching the ball. His feet had made skid marks on the damp grass. The ground looked as if a car had done an emergency stop on it.

Joshua looked briefly at Fentwood, to see whether or not he was angry. He looked strange and distracted. Joshua briefly caught his eye and looked away.

'I say, the grass here is in a shockingly bad condition,' commented the terrified writer, with the desperation of a tigress protecting her dying cub. He added, 'Everyone's entitled to an "after lunch shot". I'd take one now if I were you. I dread to think what's going to happen to me when I try my hand at it.'

Fentwood accepted Joshua's gesture. This time, his club came down so violently that a chunk of earth was hurled into the air and the ball stayed where it had been placed.

'It's all right, Sebastian. It's only a game. Now, you can watch me disgrace myself,' said Joshua kindly. He decided to play as badly as he could, for the sake of what he called 'his sweet beloved babe', and because of his terror of being forced back to his typewriter too early.

He took out a long-distance iron club from his bag, knowing that Fentwood was fixing him with a glacial stare. He was so nervous that he bent over to untie his shoelaces, to give himself a chance to tie them up again. He stood up, pushed his cap to the back of his head and leaned forward to hit the ball.

'Wish me luck, Sebastian,' he said half-wittedly.

Joshua thought he could hear Rita's voice. He sometimes felt that, despite her occasionally cutting remarks, she was watching him and loved him from wherever she was.

'Whatever you do, miss that ball, Joshua, if you don't want to lose the baby. Swing the golf club as hard as you can but see that it passes at least an inch above the ball.'

Joshua spoke to her out loud but not loudly enough to enable Fentwood to hear what he was saying. 'I might not get it right. The club will hit the ball accidentally and it will be such a good shot that it will cause me to get the sack and make me touch the poison, the ink, that will kill the baby. Then I might end up in a bloody mental institution.'

'Do you usually talk to yourself while you're teeing up?' asked Fentwood irritably.

'Oh, sorry. I'll start now. It's just that I'm such a terrible player.'

Joshua lifted his club. He aimed for the air, an inch above the ball. His desire to please Fentwood was so strong that it made him feel sick.

His plan went wrong. His club landed on the ball, which flew through the air like a rocket. It landed on the edge of the green just above the bunker. He was about to break into a subconscious rendering of *Donald the Dub* but bit into his tongue in panic.

Fentwood looked at the ground and was reminded once more of the mere five feet which separated the top of his head from it. He lurched over to Joshua.

'I suppose that was just luck,' he said coldly.

'It was. I can't understand it. I've always been a very bad player.'

'I'm getting bored here,' said Fentwood. 'I want to go back to the office. I've got nothing on for the rest of the weekend. Can you do some more work with the metal strips?'

Joshua was terrified of refusing Fentwood's request but a bold streak in him told him that he was being taken advantage of. It hurt his pride to feel blackmailed. Had he said 'no' to Fentwood, he would have risked his very soul.

'I'll certainly come back with you if you need my help. It would be a pleasure,' he began. 'The only thing is, I've got a family and I like to be with them whenever I can. I could ring home and say I'll be out all day, if you really want me to.'

'You don't have to if you don't want to,' said Fentwood in a hostile tone.

'Oh, no. Sometimes, one has to put duty before family life. I'd like to come back.'

'Good,' exclaimed Fentwood. There was no sign of appreciation in his voice. He sounded as if he thought of Joshua as his slave, his chattel, his cur.

Joshua was afraid of giving Fentwood a lift in Rita's Porsche which he had parked outside the golf club. He decided to collect it later. He rang for a minicab. There was a lot of traffic, due to roadworks. It took him and Fentwood two hours to get from outer London to Jermyn Street.

The taxi driver, a silver-toothed, brawny Negro, told his passengers what they owed him. Fentwood leant back and closed his eyes. Joshua paid the fifty pound fare.

Fentwood opened the door of the offices, without speaking to Joshua. Joshua felt that he was being so badly treated that he planned to take a particularly nasty form of revenge on his boss, once Lucinda had died.

It did not surprise him that other staff members had been reluctantly persuaded to work that day. He wondered how much these people were being paid for their sweatshop-style labour.

'I've got the boxes in my office, Joshua. Come over in about half an hour,' commanded Fentwood. There was neither grace nor gratitude in his tone of voice.

Joshua despised bullies. The other staff, who had been ordered to come in that Saturday without pay, also felt exploited. After half an hour had passed, he went into Fentwood's office.

'Take a look at the metal strips in the first box, will you,' commanded Fentwood. The metal strips, which Joshua had begun to put in the right order, had been tampered with. The Ds had been mixed up with the As and the Bs. Fentwood had tampered with them, because he was bitter about his height, as opposed to Joshua's height. He was also infuriated because Joshua was a much better golfer than he.

'I thought you'd got it right, Flinton,' (no longer Joshua) he said. 'The first quarter of these strips are not in alphabetical order at all, contrary to what I was given to believe.'

'I'd spent hours arranging them. Why aren't they in order?' asked Joshua, suspiciously.

'Because you didn't bother to do your job properly!' exclaimed Fentwood angrily.

'I'm not a fool. These strips have been scuttled,' ventured Joshua courageously.

Fentwood flew into a rage. 'No one's scuttled them. It seems as if you don't know your alphabet.'

'I'm not taking this!' said Joshua bravely.

'You are taking anything I choose to give to you. Stand up on the chair over there and recite the alphabet from A to Z.' He wanted to see whether or not his employee would obey him. He assumed that he would and was not surprised when he got up onto the chair and stood up straight.

Fentwood went up to Joshua and blew foul breath into his face, making him gag. He went out to the main office and called the staff members into his room, before making a short speech.

'This man, Flinton, has wasted hours and hours of my time and the firm's money. He has been given the simple task of arranging metal strips in alphabetical order. He appears to think that D comes before B. Well, Flinton, recite the alphabet. Come on. We're all ears.'

'Are you quite sure that this is what you want me to do, sir?'

'Yes it is!' shouted Fentwood.

A number of staff members had become convinced that Fentwood was mad. Some of them sniggered surreptitiously. They all supported Joshua and were sorry for him.

'I shall certainly recite the alphabet, sir,' said Joshua. 'When I do, you're going to regret having asked me to do so.'

Joshua's fear of dismissal had turned to a dramatic feeling of relief. He felt another, much more pronounced surge of mania gush through him. It was as if his whole body were on fire.

'Ready, sir?' he asked, his voice raised. 'Here comes the alphabet. Since it is your wish, I shall recite it from A, as in apple, through to Z, as in Zhivago.'

'All right. Bloody well get on with it, Flinton!' shouted Fentwood.

Joshua then felt as if he were floating in space, even though he hadn't taken his 'running sweets' that day. This often happened to him whenever insanity hit him. He broke into raucous song.

'A' is for arseholes, all tattered and torn.
'Heigh-ho,' said Rowley.
'B's for the bugger who's never been born,
With a roly-poly up 'em and stuff 'em,
'Heigh-ho,' said Anthony Rowley.
'C' is for —

Fentwood interrupted Joshua. 'I order you to stop singing that filthy, disgusting song, Flinton!' he shouted.

Joshua ignored him. A few of Fentwood's employees smiled broadly at him. Some of them winked at him. Joshua felt elated because of the support he was receiving from his fellow employees. He continued, until the last verse:

'W's for whore who makes fucking a farce.
'Heigh-ho,' said Rowley.
And X, Y and Z you can shove up your arse!
With a roly-poly up 'em and stuff 'em,
'Heigh-ho,' said Anthony Rowley.

Suddenly, many of the staff members left Fentwood's office, like a crowd of people seeking an air-raid shelter, or a flurry of journalists racing from a gory court case, desperate to ring up their newspapers. The reason for their leaving was their aversion to seeing Joshua being humiliated.

Fentwood was sitting with his legs crossed at right angles. He was dumbfounded but forced himself not to show it.

'What's my phone doing off the hook, Flinton?' he shouted.

'It was your call, not mine, that came through while I was singing, and you left it on hold, sir.' Joshua was too proud to fight dismissal any more.

The caller was Fentwood's former mother-in-law, whom

179

he respected and was very much in awe of. He had lifted the receiver and was so shocked by Joshua's singing that he accidentally failed to replace it. His former mother-in-law had heard the whole song.

'Pack your belongings and get out of here, Flinton,' said Fentwood. 'That song was nothing short of revolting.'

'I might consider leaving when you give me back my fifty pounds for the taxi fare from the golf club to these offices,' said Joshua assertively.

'I don't owe it to you. You're rubbish. Get out!'

'You *do* owe it to me, on top of a whole month's wages.'

'I've just told you to get out.'

'What if I called the Law? What if I called my solicitor?'

'No contract was signed, even before I came here,' said Fentwood. 'I'm not giving you so much as a penny.'

'You're stupid, as well as being a dwarf and a lousy golfer. My contract is in my briefcase. It was signed by Mr Hills, who was level-headed and not a grotesque, twisted schizo like you. Here's a copy.'

Fentwood snatched the copy from Joshua's hand. 'No need to panic, Pint Size,' shouted Joshua at the top of his voice, adding, 'I've got two more copies of it, one in my solicitor's office and one at my house. Sounds a bit like check-matey-kins, doesn't it, old boy? The money for a whole month's wages, as well as the taxi fare is coming to me but, as I've got such a nice, gentle nature, I'll leave you just enough money to buy yourself a pair of stilts. They might change your attitude towards other people who are taller than you!'

Fentwood stared at Joshua aghast.

'There's just one other thing, sir,' said Joshua. 'You're so ignorant, you haven't got the faintest idea who I am, have you?'

'I'm not interested in who you are.'

'Whether you are or not, I'll tell you who I am. I am

Joshua Flinton, a best-selling writer. Here's one of my books.' Joshua took one of his books from his briefcase. 'Take a look at my picture. The inside jacket states how many books I've written. There's worse to come, I'm afraid, Half Pint. As a celebrity, I could go to any newspaper of my choice and spill the story about your twisted cruelty to innocent people. I get sad when others make crass, oafish louts of themselves. Don't think I worked here for my living. I worked here in order to get what I call "book fodder". I've got a blockbuster on you and I'm going to use your name.'

Fentwood continued to stare at Joshua, with his mouth wide open in shock.

'On principle, because I'm wealthy and world-famous, I'm suing you and I'm going to win,' said Joshua. He continued, 'It's not myself I care about. It's the ones who are kicked while they are lying in the gutter and can't hit back. I refer in particular to the poor old tea lady to whom you were so rude the other morning. I am, and always have been, a representative of the underdog.'

'I order you to leave,' said Fentwood icily as he grated his teeth.

'That's what I intend to do. In fairness to the weaker victims of your despicable, caddish behaviour, the police and my lawyers will be visiting you on my behalf. It's been nice knowing you, Tom Thumb.'

When Joshua had stormed out of the offices in Jermyn Street, Fentwood picked up a valuable glass paperweight and hurled it against the wall, smashing it. He opened his desk in which there was some Cognac and took two swigs from the bottle.

Joshua feared, once more, that he would be prematurely dragged back to his 'liquor', in the form of his typewriter, although he felt proud of turning on Fentwood and having the courage of his convictions. Even the event of his being tortured and tormented by his work was not as awesome to him as the fear that he could have been seen to be a coward. However, he knew he would have continued to suck up to Fentwood, had the tyrant not scuttled the metal strips. He also knew that, as he thought mainly of himself, he would have failed to defend the rights of other staff members too weak to hit back.

Joshua shuddered as a wave of nausea, guilt and shame surged through him. He knew that fundamentally he was a coward, as his beloved Rita had told him on several occasions.

A museum, namely a large house on the far side of Hampstead Heath, where Rita and her younger brother Edward had been born and bred, had just been done up to commemorate her life and work. It was a Bath stone premises, containing harpsichords, pianos and other musical instruments. The walls were covered from top to bottom with flattering pictures of Rita, accentuating her lustrous, long red hair and sparkling green eyes. The lawns surrounding the museum gave it a pleasant, rustic look.

The curator of the museum had written to Joshua and asked him to open it and cut a piece of pink ribbon across its front door, after making a short speech.

'How do you feel about this, little brother?' asked Charles one morning at breakfast.

'I'm not up to it. I just can't do it.'

'Can't you have a few drinks and take some of your precious pills before you do it? All you will have to do will be to make a short speech and cut the ribbon. I'd think you were awfully wet if you refused.'

'OK, I'll do it,' said Joshua reluctantly, 'just to please you as you've been so good to me since we grew up.'

'Well done, little brother. If you aren't well on the day concerned, I'll do it instead of you.'

Joshua took plenty of 'running sweets'. Charles drove

him up the museum's drive in Rita's Porsche and let him out.

'It'll be OK, little brother, as long as you don't start talking about fucking Russian literature to anyone. If you do do that, I'll come over to you and give you a good crack.'

'Trust me. I won't do it, Charles,' said Joshua.

A large crowd had gathered, as well as a sea of newspaper reporters. Joshua approached the front door of the museum, waving and smiling. A pair of scissors was placed into his hand by the curator. He began to speak.

'It is an honour to see so many people who came here today, just to watch me open this museum. I have accepted the invitation to do so because of how very much my late aunt, Rita Flinton, meant to me, not only because of her beauty and talent, but also because of her brilliant wit and kindness, particularly when I had just lost my father.'

Joshua allowed the blades of the scissors to go on either side of the ribbon. The scissors were blunt. He tried to cut the ribbon three times. The 'running sweets', which he had taken earlier, were making him disinhibited. His mania returned. He turned towards Charles, who was standing close to the front door, with his face flushed and his head lowered in embarrassment.

Joshua then turned to the curator and assumed that the blunt scissors had been given to him as a practical joke. The cameramen saw the rage in his face and held up their cameras, hoping for an embarrassing scene.

'Look here, you bastard! You deliberately gave me blunt scissors in order to make a fool of me. You've only made a fool of yourself. This is no way to treat a distinguished gentleman of letters!' shouted Joshua.

Every member of his audience laughed at him, except Charles.

They had laughed at Joshua because it was apparent in his speech that he lacked style and panache.

Charles walked towards him.

'Come on, little brother. It wasn't your fault, this time. Just walk through the crowd, smiling and waving.'

Joshua was euphoric because of the 'running sweets' he had taken, and by the fact that he had such a wonderful brother.

'Would you like me to come to the golf course with you? It would do you good to play a few holes,' suggested Charles.

'No. I'd like to go alone,' said Joshua, adding, 'I'm so lucky to have a brother like you.'

'Oh, don't talk daft,' said Charles. He continued, 'I treated you appallingly when we were children, as I've said many times before and I also committed malicious arson. I'm just trying to make up for that.'

Joshua found out that the museum did not open until nine o'clock in the morning. His mania had plummeted into a depression which was so acute that he could barely speak. Even Charles's joviality and continuous cracking of jokes failed to make him laugh. Charles was concerned, but was determined not to be intrusive. Anxious, earnest questions were asked by Arthur, Nanny Marion and Charles, out of Joshua's hearing. Joshua's depression was at its worst. He knew his mood was upsetting his family and he decided that he did not wish to go on living.

He got up at six o'clock one morning and had two baths, one after the other, followed by three showers. He cleaned his teeth five times. There was a piece of rope about six yards long in the boot of Rita's Porsche. The key was still in the ignition. He got in and drove to the museum. He thought it would be an honour to die in a place dedicated to the goddess from whom he had moulded most of Lucinda

Maloney, and the thought gave him courage.

He went up to the front door which had a glass panel. He took off one of his shoes, to enable him to break the glass. He let himself in with the indoor handle, carrying the coil of rope which he had taken from the boot of the car.

He was faced by a grand staircase, dividing at the top. He walked slowly towards the top of the stairs, as a criminal would to the scaffold.

He tied the rope to the rung of one of the bannisters but was too incompetent to be able to make a noose.

He decided to tie the noose with his shoelaces instead of the rope which he threw to the floor. He put the loop round his neck and climbed over the banister from which he intended to fall to his death.

He was convinced that a jinx had descended on his book, preventing him from killing Lucinda. He would be losing his life for the heroine in a book, whom an unknown force was not allowing him to kill, purify, and finally exorcise.

He noticed that there was a drop of about thirty feet. He did not brood before he jumped. He wanted his death to be quick as every second tortured him.

He jumped. He had not tied the noose correctly. The shoelaces coiling round his neck, failed to tighten. He fell to the floor and lay on his back. Strangely, he was not injured. Then he went upstairs to repeat the procedure again.

He tied the shoelaces to the bannister rung, as he had before, and then wondered whether it would be more practical if he were to go to the top of the building and throw himself off the roof onto the flagstones below.

He realized that this would be blasphemous, however, as the building was being used as a museum to commemorate Rita, his excitingly waspish deity. Further, he reasoned that it would be grossly disrespectful to her memory to spatter the flagstones with his blood because it would be impossible to scrub them clean.

He put his shoelaces round his neck again and was about to jump from the bannister rung once more. A cleaner, her hair in curlers, carrying a mop and bumper, scurried across the hall. It was clear that she was late for duty as she was looking anxiously at her watch. She was talking out loud.

'Bloody hell, I cleaned this side yesterday. I'll go over and do the other side.'

It was Joshua who saw her first. Had she seen him first, she might have had a heart attack.

'I say,' began Joshua, who was standing on the outer part of the staircase.

The cleaner whitened and was speechless.

'I say, I'm sorry I startled you. I'm not mad. I'm just a perfectly normal, harmless bloke. There's no need to be afraid of me. I've reached the end of my life and, for want of better words, I've come here to dispatch myself.'

The cleaner ran to the back of the building, screaming. She left her mop and bumper in the hall. It occurred to Joshua that if she reported him to anyone he might be sectioned under the Mental Health Act. This was something he feared more than anything else in the world, even his failure to kill Lucinda. He jumped to the floor and ran outside onto the lawn.

It was raining heavily. He walked backwards, so that he could get a complete view of the house. He knelt down on the lawn and allowed the torrential rain to soak through his hair and clothes. He spoke out loud as if uttering a prayer. The tone of his voice conveyed a grief so intense, that his words would have deeply shocked anyone hearing them. Their delivery was slow and despairing but his voice was loud, much louder than his usual voice.

186

Once upon a midnight dreary, while I pondered, weak and weary,
Over many a quaint and curious volume of forgotten lore.

'Come on home, little brother.'

Charles had surprised him by coming up behind him and tapping him on the shoulder.

'Charles! How did you know I was here?'

'Finding you wasn't too difficult. Some cleaner saw you and got me out. It was lucky I came. Otherwise you could have been binned. Dr Pittas has gone away on leave and there's an American psychiatrist taking over his practice while he's away. He's a nice man. I rang him up and talked to him about your case, and he said he'd be happy to see you at two-thirty this afternoon. What medication are you taking? I can't remember.'

'The stimulants, that is to say my "running sweets", which all my doctors have prescribed for me, but I no longer take my epilepsy pills because they make me feel tired. So does the Chlorpromazine.'

'Fair enough. When did you last have an epileptic fit?'

'Eighteen months ago.'

'Jolly hockey sticks!' exclaimed Charles, in a strong public school accent, imitating his brother's voice. (He intended to humour him.)

Dr Zett Rubrick was the name of the American psychiatrist whom Joshua was due to see, accompanied by Charles. He had a strong Boston accent. He was an amiable man who lacked inhibitions. He was slight in build, bald as a billiard ball and looked like Khrushchev.* He was startlingly 'up front', in a 'common sense' sort of way. Though outspoken, it was impossible not to like him.

*Khrushchev was president of the Soviet Union after Stalin's death.

187

'Oh, hi! Which one of you two guys is Joshua?' he asked.

'He is,' said Charles. 'We'd like to be in the consulting room together, as I know everything there is to know about my brother, more than he knows himself.'

'Is that so? Why don't you two guys sit down? Do you like the Venetian blinds open or shut?'

'Shut, please,' said the two brothers in unison.

'Now, Joshua,' said Rubrick, 'I've made some preliminary notes and have read your casenotes which Dr Pittas left here. I know all about you. Things seem to amount to an imaginary woman, whom you've created in your own mind, but can't bump off because she is only a fictitious character and is understandably unreal. She haunts you, doesn't she?'

'Yes, she does,' said Joshua.

The doctor continued, 'Her presence in your book is so sacred to you that you can't bear thinking about her because she's not there for you, so you want to kill her off.'

'That's right.'

'Have you ever had girlfriends?'

'Only one-night stands. I pick up women in pubs. I also pick up prostitutes. I go for redheads with long hair. I go back to their rooms or alleyways and I pretend they are my heroine.'

'How do you feel each time?'

'During the sex act I feel pretty good. Afterwards, I feel awful.'

'That's quite normal. A man always gets depressed, once he's shot his load,' Rubrick said vulgarly. 'Also, you know you've had a street woman and that she'll never be a replacement for your muse. I'd like to hear your own version of what you did this morning.'

Joshua told the doctor about the rope and the shoelaces, described the cleaning woman and his leaving the house.

188

'You quit the house when it was raining hard, didn't you?' said Rubrick.

Joshua spoke with a deep, sepulchral voice. His gloom made his delivery unnaturally slow.

'Yes. I knelt down on the wet earth and I recited *The Raven.*'

'So what?' said Rubrick, almost angrily. He sometimes spoke abrasively to his patients, particularly if they appeared intensely troubled. He found that in eighty per cent of cases, the technique was the equivalent of slapping someone's face.

Very suddenly and without warning, Joshua laughed uproariously. It was as if a blood-sucking leech had been clawed off his body.

'This certainly has been a promising visit,' said Rubrick. 'Do you want to come back next Wednesday at two-thirty?'

'We'll be here,' said Charles. 'Thank you so much for making Joshua laugh. It's more than his family can do.'

Dr Rubrick wrote out a prescription for more of the 'running sweets' which Joshua needed.

The brothers kept the appointment with him the following week.

'How are you feeling, Joshua?' asked the chirpy American psychiatrist.

'Oh, he's ever so much better. Since you said "so what?" last week, he's been laughing so much that he's been falling all over the house. Also, his appetite has come back.'

'I wasn't asking you. I was asking Joshua.'

'Well, I'm still not quite right,' said Joshua. 'I feel more relaxed about the book, though, and although it's difficult for me to kill my heroine, I think I might try again. I don't feel suicidal any more.'

Rubrick drew on his blotting paper. Unbeknown to the brothers, he was sketching them. He portrayed Charles as looking serious, worried and gaunt. Joshua looked broader in the face and determined to do what he had to do.

'Have you ever taken antidepressants, Joshua?' asked Rubrick.

'No. Only Dexamphetamine Sulphate. That is to say the highly successful stimulant that my other doctors have been prescribing for me. I like to call these pills my "running sweets".'

'I see. I'm going to prescribe for you a well-known antidepressant called Prozac. It will cater for your obsessive compulsive disorder as well as your depression. Just take one every morning. The pills will take about six weeks to work and during that time you'll feel tired as they lower the blood pressure. Do you want to try them?'

'Yes. If you think they will do me any good.'

'It will help you considerably, I guess,' said Rubrick. 'Prozac doesn't interfere with the stimulants you call your "running sweets" which you are taking, I will continue to prescribe them for you.'

'I'll take the Prozac. I'd be prepared to try anything in the world to enable me to kill that woman. I hope that killing her will purify my soul and hers for the rest of eternity,' cried Joshua passionately.

'Good on you, Flinton,' said the psychiatrist who addressed him by his surname as a form of splashing him with cold water.

'I think I can trust you to make me kill her,' said Joshua after a pause.

'I know so. Sooner or later, you'll be likely to find a nice girl who will look after you. Are you aware of Oscar Wilde's words, *For each man kills the thing he loves.*'

'Yes. They haunt me all the time.'

Rubrick used a strange expression for an American. He liked to surprise his patients by the use of English slang, delivered with a phoney English accent.

'You're going to leg it, Flinton. I know it in my bones. Right, Charles?'

'Right, Dr Rubrick,' said Charles.

It was a warm sunny morning in May. Joshua had started the Prozac but had not got to the stage of feeling tired. He decided to take the train from Paddington Station. He wanted to spend the whole day playing golf at a golf course near Reading. He carried his clubs over his left shoulder. He held his mobile phone in his right hand.

Charles came downstairs while he was opening the front door.

'You're playing golf, I see. That shows you're feeling better. Where are you playing?'

At a golf course near Reading. I'm getting the train from Paddington.'

'Not Gadhampton, this time?'

'No, I don't want to be reminded of Sebastian Fentwood.'

'Do you want me to drive you to the golf course in Rita's Porsche?'

'It's OK. I'd prefer to go by train so that I can look at the countryside.'

The train was not crowded. It was divided into open compartments. Joshua travelled first class. He sat near the window and showed his ticket to the ticket collector. He put his golf clubs on the floor and rested his feet on a copy of the *Daily Express*, on the seat facing him.

The green countryside enchanted him and had a hypnotic effect on him.

In the next open compartment sat a middle-aged man who was the Duke of Pendlebury, whose large family had moved from Northamptonshire to Berkshire where his mother was terminally ill. The Duke was stiff-looking and balding.

He had been a colonel during World War II and was wearing a jacket awash with a sea of medals; he wore it wherever he went. As smoking had been banned on trains, the Duke took snuff.

His valet sat next to him. The Duke occasionally made benign remarks about the weather.

Suddenly, a surge of mania flowed through Joshua. He had just taken a handful of 'running sweets'. This was the perfect time to kill Lucinda, to prevent her from haunting him any more.

He regretted the absence of his typewriter but took advantage of his mobile phone. He dialled his secretary's number with difficulty because his hands were shaking.

'Miss Jones!' (He always addressed her in this old-fashioned manner. It was part of his sense of humour. Her name was not Miss Jones; it was Mrs Cradsbrook.) 'Oh, God, Miss Jones, are you there?'

Joshua was unaware that he was shouting at the top of his voice.

'It's all right. I'm here, sir,' said Mrs Cradsbrook. Her tone was extremely formal.

'I think I can do it! It's suddenly come to me. I can kill her. I'll do it, now! Have you got a copy of my manuscript in front of you?'

'I'll get it up on the computer now, sir.'

'Good. We'll lead up to it, briefly. Then, we'll kill her.' Joshua still did not realize that he was shouting at the top of his voice.

The Duke, sitting in the other compartment, became curious and wondered whether or not the man whom he could not see was a psychopath. He did not wish to speak to him, for fear of getting killed himself.

'OK, Miss Jones, we're on page 257 where the two lovers, Lucinda and Ferdinando, both about to die of AIDS, have steamy, ear-splitting sex in two different ways

192

in a disused graveyard. As they both have tuberculosis, they cough blood violently during their orgasms.'

The Duke cleared his throat.

'I say, Your Grace, do you think I ought to go over to that man and tell him to lower his voice?' said his valet.

'Certainly not! He may be armed. Most of his conversation suggests that he is mad and dangerous. One doesn't talk about killing someone and then discuss lurid sex at the top of one's voice, does one?' said the Duke.

'No, indeed one doesn't, Your Grace.'

Joshua continued to dictate. He said, 'Let's go back a bit.'

*'I'll lie on my back on this gravestone. I want you to lie the other way on top of me so that I can lick your clitoris,' said Ferdinando,' adding, 'we'll have soixante-neuf first.' Then we'll have fellatio.**

Joshua was getting even more nervous and his voice rose to a clipped military bark.

Ferdinando repeated, 'We'll have top to bottom sex and oral sex, one after the other. Take my cock, full stop,' said *Ferdinando. 'When it's hard,* comma, *try to get it into your mouth,* full stop.

'Oh, Christ, comma, *this is pure nectar. Get your head up quick before I come down your throat and choke you,* full stop.'

'Could you please read that again, Miss Jones?'

'You've just said, "*Get your head up quick before I come down your throat and choke you, full stop.*"'

'Oh, no, no, no and sons limited. We can't have a full

<hr>

* *Soixante-neuf*: sixty-nine: a somewhat ribald French expression which is self-explanatory.

stop after *choke you.* What we need here is a bleeding exclamation mark!'

Joshua raised his head while dictating. He saw a man in a black suit, matching waistcoat, white shirt and black bow tie, standing staring at him, looking baffled. The man had light brown hair, cut in a short back and sides. He looked nondescript.

'Sir!' exclaimed the stranger.

'Who are you and what the devil do you want?' shouted Joshua.

'I have the honour to serve His Grace, the Duke of Pendlebury. He is on his way to Berkshire where his mother is terminally ill.'

'Is that any business of mine?'

'I have come to ask you to stop your disgusting telephone conversation.'

'Oh, piss off, you silly old boot!' said Joshua.

He continued the phone call, and repeated his words.

'That's it,' said the valet. 'If you utter one more word on your telephone, I'm calling the guard because you are upsetting His Grace.'

'Stuff His fucking Grace!' shouted Joshua. The valet ignored him and returned to his seat.

'What sort of a man is he?' asked the Duke. 'How is he dressed?'

'He's wearing a bright red sweater, tweed plus-fours and a matching tweed cap. His socks are red to match his sweater. When he was dictating, he was holding his mobile telephone in his right hand and was waving a golf club in the air with his left. In other words, his speech and actions are somewhat singular, Your Grace,' said the valet, adding, 'His eyes are rolling about in their sockets like those of a mad Russian who's just lost all his roubles.'

Joshua was on the verge of tears. He had been so close

to killing Lucinda and would have done so, had he not been interrupted.

He had to walk past the Duke to go to the lavatory. The Duke caught his eye.

'I say, I was enjoying your raunchy dictation to that secretary of yours, what!'*

Joshua flushed to the roots of his hair. 'I am most indebted to you, Your Grace,' he muttered sycophantically.

Joshua was very sad on returning to London. Every time he was within an inch of killing Lucinda, he was thwarted. He wondered whether he had actually killed her without his knowledge, in many different ways, but she still would not stay dead.

Charles met his brother at Paddington Station.

'What is it, little brother? I'm sure it's not the end of the world. Something came between you and the killing of Lucinda Maloney, didn't it?'

'Yes. She still will *not* die. When I think I've killed her, she won't stay dead.'

'We're not giving up, Joshua. We're going to leg it, like Dr Rubrick said, and we're going to start tomorrow. I know a quiet hotel called the Admiral Nelson near Launceston Castle in Cornwall. You must remember it. Perhaps you were too young. We went there when we were children. We'll go there together so that you don't start any of your bloody nonsense. The owners of the hotel are a bit eccentric, as you will probably remember, but at least it's peaceful and you'll have me there to give you moral support if you get distressed about your writing.'

The brothers travelled from London to Cornwall in Rita's

---

*The author had a similar experience, but the Duke of Pendlebury was Prince Philip, the Duke of Edinburgh. She had to raise her voice because her secretary, Mave, was extremely deaf. She was writing *The Rendon Boy to the Grave Is Gone*, which was later entitled *Stop the Car, Mr Becket*.

Porsche. Charles had rung up the hotel and asked if he and his brother could stay there for a few days. It was the manager, Jack Menhenniot, who had taken the call.

'Oh, aye, of course you can come. Do you want to share a room?'

'I'd rather not,' said Charles mildly.

'In that case, we can give you two separate rooms. I'm afraid they're at the opposite ends of the hotel.'

'That's fine. In fact, it's excellent,' said Charles. He sounded distinctly relieved.

'What's your name, sir?'

'Charles Flinton. My brother is Joshua Flinton, the writer.'

Menhenniot did not appear to have heard of Joshua Flinton.

'When will you come?' he asked.

'Tomorrow, at five o'clock.'

'Where are you from?'

'London.'

'Oh. Oh, I see.' Menhenniot sounded disapproving, as if he disliked people from London. He then told his slatternly wife, who had come from the bar to the hall, that his two visitors would be travelling from London.

The brothers arrived at the hotel in Rita's Porsche. Charles found it a depressing place, made worse by its dark, chipped, slated roof. It had once been a smart-looking hotel, but it appeared as if it had gone to seed.

Charles rang the bell. The door was opened by Menhenniot, a fat, slovenly man with breath that stank like a rotting carcase. He ushered the brothers to the reception desk.

A sluttish-looking woman came out from a side door and stood by Menhenniot's side. She was Mrs Menhenniot. She had an intimidating look about her. Her behaviour

196

was often xenophobic whenever she met anyone from London. Like her husband, her standards of dental hygiene were poor.

'The hotel's very crowded at this time of year but my husband and I have managed to fit you in. One of you can go into room sixteen and the other can go into room twenty-seven,' she said.

Joshua went into room sixteen, a gloomy room, overlooking a narrow street. He had two baths, one after the other and cleaned his teeth four times. He got out his typewriter, fed in paper and took a palmful of 'running sweets', to prepare himself for his task. He lay on his back on the bed and waited for the 'running sweets' to work.

It was almost two o'clock in the morning. He had a third bath and started typing. He fought his fear that he would never be able to kill his heroine. He took yet another palmful of 'running sweets'.

Try as he did, he was unable to kill Lucinda, because part of him wanted her to stay alive. The 'running sweets', which Dr Bennett, Dr Pittas and Dr Rubrick had prescribed for him in bulk, took away his inhibitions. He screamed at the top of his voice. 'I'm trying to kill you but you won't stay dead! Why are you so cruel to the one who begat you? I'm trying to control you, so why won't you be controlled?'

Joshua was unaware of the fact that Mr and Mrs Menhenniot occupied the room next door, divided from room sixteen by a thin wall. He went over to the window and ripped down the curtains in frustration. He went into the bathroom and coiled the cord which had supported them round the radiator which was boiling, even though it was still May and the weather was quite warm.

'Can't you go with grace? Can you not stop persecuting me?' shouted Joshua. He wrenched the radiator from the wall in a demented rage, causing boiling water to gush through the room, under the door and down the stairs.

Mrs Menhenniot was more courageous than her husband. She opened the door of room sixteen with a skeleton key. She was wearing an unwashed dressing gown, covered with food and beer stains.

'Have you gone raving mad?' she shouted.

'As a matter of fact, no. I have merely taken the liberty of selecting an altered state.'

'What do you mean, you've merely taken the liberty of selecting an altered state?'

'You wouldn't understand. I'm trying to kill her but she won't stay dead. Every time I try to kill her, my typewriter keys get jammed! I'm writing a book called *The Killing of Lucinda Maloney*, which is disturbing me more than I can say in words, because I yearn to kill her although I haven't got the guts to do so.'

Mrs Menhenniot was terrified.

'I'm afraid I'll have to fetch my husband,' she muttered.

Menhenniot had sunk into an inebriated stupor. He was wearing ear plugs and his wife was unable to wake him up. 'Wake up, you idle slob!' she shouted, but her words fell on deaf ears. She went back into room sixteen.

'You've flooded this bloody hotel!' she screamed at the top of her voice.

'You're making far, far too much noise!' shouted Joshua. 'You can't go into hotel rooms at two o'clock in the morning and cause a breach of the peace. Do you realize Edgar Allan Poe's mother-in-law slept peacefully in her bed while he was writing *The Raven*?'

'Lord save us! Is he staying in this hotel?' asked the petrified woman.

'No, of course he bloody isn't! He croaked in eighteen forty-nine. Go back to bed. You're making too much noise.'

'*I'm* making too much noise?'

'Yes, you are.'

'You're a raving lunatic. I'm calling the police.'

'Not until I've got hold of my fucking psychiatrist. I've got my mobile phone with me.'

'You've wrenched the land phone from the wall!' yelled Mrs Menhenniot.

'I know, I ripped the phone from the wall, to stop you getting the police out.'

There was a long corridor outside room sixteen. Couples in dressing gowns poured out of their rooms in droves.

'Shut up!' an elderly woman said.

'You shut up!' said Joshua. 'You just can't make a fiendish racket like this at this time of night. Shut up, I tell you!'

'*You're* making all the noise. *You* shut up,' said the occupants of the corridor in unison, like a congregation saying responses in church.

Mrs Menhenniot could take no more. The sight of the water from the radiator seeping over the floor of room sixteen and down the stairs, was such a shock to her that she forced herself to erase it from her mind. She went into the bedroom which she shared with her husband and took a sleeping pill. The following morning she took Charles aside and told him about Joshua's behaviour.

She saw Charles and Joshua in the reception area later on before they were due to leave. Charles, who was intensely embarrassed by her description of his brother's behaviour, paid the bill by cheque, with his head bowed and his pen shaking in his hand.

The brothers were the first customers to leave the hotel. Mrs Menhenniot followed them to Rita's Porsche, as was her habit when anyone left, regardless of their conduct.

'Mind you, she's not very attractive,' said Joshua loudly. 'She's obese. She's dirty; she's got foul breath and on top of that, she's got amazing B.O.'

'Shut your bleeding hole! She's standing three feet

away,' said Charles in a hoarse whisper. Mrs Menhenniot was humiliated. She staggered back to the hotel, wondering how she would be able to call the police when the hotel's phone had been ripped from its socket.

Charles opened the driver's door of Rita's Porsche and got in. He put on his driving gloves and a pair of pilot's goggles to remind himself of Ian Fleming's books.

'Come on, little brother, in you get,' he commanded.

'Where are you going?'

'Back to London. Where do you think we're going?'

'I'm staying here.'

'Why? You'd be better off coming with me.'

'I can't go anywhere until I've killed Lucinda Maloney. I've got to finish off what I've started.'

'You mean you want to go back to that hotel – where you disgraced yourself?'

'No. Of course not. I'll find another hotel.'

'Don't be stupid. Don't you realize, you'll never be able to kill Lucinda unless you kill yourself first.'

'Why, Charles?'

'You must know why. The bloody woman's a part of you. She lives inside you. Are you coming back to London with me, or are you going to stay here and get arrested?'

'I'm not coming, Charles. I'm afraid I already knew the truth before you told me.'

'Get in the car, you fucking fool! The Law's coming,' shouted Charles at the top of his voice. He started revving the engine.

'No. I'll need two days to think for a while. Then I'll come back to London. I'll get the train.'

Joshua realized that he would never be able to kill Lucinda Maloney. He had known all along but had forced himself to deny the fact that her abandoned spirit lived within him and would never leave him until he died. He thought once more about Flaubert's words, 'I *am* Madame

Bovary.' He and Lucinda would grow old together and die together.

He decided he would get on with other books and try to kill Lucinda at a later date. He had left a typed note on the floor of room sixteen. In the note, he admitted his folly and failure.

TO ALL THOSE MISGUIDED ENOUGH TO WRITE FOR A LIVING

Do not allow yourself to fall in love with your main protagonist. You may think you are in control but you are not. In the case of a male writer, your main protagonist is as addictive as heroin. She will run away from you and you will not catch her. You will be like Dante trying to reach Beatrice. You may spend the rest of your life looking for her but you will not find her. In the end, you will know the reason. She lives inside you. She is part of you. She will grow old with you and she will die with you. She is a cancerous tumour. Once her claws get hold of you, she won't let you go till you croak. That is precisely what the book, 'The Killing of Lucinda Maloney' is doing to me.

No one knew what Joshua did after Charles's departure. No one knew where he went. Ponds, lakes and coastlines were dragged. The police searched day and night and found no one. The local moorlands, as well as the whole of Dartmoor were scoured with the help of Alsatian dogs.

Charles cried every day and made irritatingly repetitive phone calls to the West Country police, asking them whether they had found his brother, but to no avail.

Eight months passed. Joshua was never found. His doting nephew, Arthur, was heartbroken by the likelihood that his uncle was dead. Arthur had inherited his uncle's promiscuity. He had had unprotected sex with a dark-haired, temperamental girl, whom he had met fleetingly in a pub. Her name was Judith Davies. She became pregnant. She was two years younger than Arthur. He was an honourable person, however, and offered to pay for her to have an abortion. She refused on the grounds that she loved children, so Arthur proposed to her, as he, too, wanted to raise a family, irrespective of the difficult woman whom he was going to marry.

After Joshua had disgraced himself in the Admiral Nelson Hotel, Judith had given birth to two twin babies on whom her husband doted.

Arthur was an industrious young man and he had got a lucrative job as a weekly columnist on *The Times*. Until he and his family had visited the Admiral Nelson Hotel, he knew nothing about the events in room sixteen. Charles, his father, did not tell him, in order to prevent him from being disappointed in the uncle whom he had loved and respected so greatly.

Arthur and his family were about to leave the Admiral Nelson Hotel, following an unpleasant night in the freezing room in which his uncle had disgraced himself the previous May. Mrs Menhenniot was sitting behind the desk in the hall. Arthur had already paid the bill for one night.

'Tis not just for board and lodging, mister,' she said aggressively. 'You've already paid for that. There's also them damages done by your uncle, the basket case in room sixteen.'

'What a cruel, ruthless, tactless woman you are!' exclaimed Arthur. 'How much is it, out of interest?'

'For a smashed-up television set, curtains ruined beyond repair, carpets damaged by running hot water, some writing with a black felt pen on the whole of the bathroom wall, which can't be erased, a new radiator in the bathroom, replacing the one your mad uncle ripped out, and dents in the woodwork of the wardrobe which were made by him banging his head against it...'

'How much do I owe you?' interrupted Arthur impatiently.

'Five thousand pounds at least.'

'That's a bit steep, isn't it?' said Arthur. 'I haven't got cash and I've come to the end of my cheque book. I'll send you a cheque when we get back to London. We didn't notice any writing on the bathroom wall. Mind you, we didn't go into the bathroom because it was too damned cold. It wasn't heated, which it bloody well should have been. What did the writing say?'

'My husband took a photograph of it. You might as well keep it. We've never had a maniac like that in here since we set up.'

Mrs Menhenniot produced the photograph which was in one of the drawers of the desk in the hall. 'Here you are. You can keep it for what it's worth,' she said in a surly tone.

Arthur read it out loud. Joshua's handwriting was forward-slanting and easy to read.

Many a suitor came to her door, by the darkness befriended,
And, as he knocked and waited to hear the sound of her
footsteps,
Knew not which beat the louder, his heart or the knocker of
*iron.**

'Those are the words of Longfellow,' said Arthur casually. 'My uncle was too vulnerable to go on writing about his heroine, Lucinda Maloney. He didn't have the stomach for it, but what a kind, gentle person he was! I'm so sorry he didn't talk to me a bit more about that book.'

* *Evangeline.*

The Flintons left, carrying their babies. The snow had melted. They went back to their car which had not been damaged by the freezing weather conditions the night before. Arthur started the engine and was about to mount the steep hill towards the castle, near which the disrupted Harveys lived. He looked first at his wife, who was filing her nails, and then at his two babies who had been belted into the back seat of the car. He suddenly realized that his heart had gone completely cold.

Mini Epilogue

This book is autobiographical. When the author wrote *The Rendon Boy to the Grave is Gone*, later to be published as *Stop the Car, Mr Becket*, she became morbidly obsessed by a male character in the book. She refrains from giving details and says she very much regrets having written the book in the first place.

For further details about the above book, see:
www.eleanorberry.net
Letter to the Editor re: *Stop the Car, Mr Becket, originally The Rendon Boy to the Grave Is Gone.*